Praise for Broken Fiction

"With a writing style that is clear and concise, while also containing traces of sarcasm and a beautiful sardonic wit, Marlene Kadar tells us how it is. *Broken Fiction* is a multi-part, braided essay that marries the fictional, the known, and the imagined with philosophy and scientific and medical exploration—and poetry. In fact, the poetry is what stands out to me most—for it winds its way through the writing from beginning to end… Kadar shines here—and in the darkest moments, she shows us light."

—**Carolyne Van Der Meer**, author of *Journeywoman* and *Sensorial*

BROKEN FICTION

BROKEN FICTION

MARLENE KADAR

INANNA poetry & fiction
Toronto, Ontario, Canada
www.inanna.ca

Copyright © 2023 Marlene Kadar

Except for the use of short passages for review purposes, no part of this book may be reproduced, in part or in whole, or transmitted in any form or by any means, electronically or mechanically, including photocopying, recording, or any information or storage retrieval system, without prior permission in writing from the publisher or a licence from the Canadian Copyright Collective Agency (Access Copyright).

We gratefully acknowledge the support of the Canada Council for the Arts and the Ontario Arts Council for our publishing program. We also acknowledge the financial support of the Government of Canada.

Cover design: Val Fullard

Any references to historical events, real people, or real places are used fictitiously. Other names, characters, places and events are products of the author's imagination.

Every effort has been made to contact copyright holders; in the event of an error or omission, please notify the publisher.

Library and Archives Canada Cataloguing in Publication

Title: Broken fiction / Marlene Kadar.
Names: Kadar, Marlene, 1950- author.
Series: Inanna poetry & fiction series.
Description: Series statement: Inanna poetry & fiction | Includes bibliographical references.
Identifiers: Canadiana (print) 20230206212 | Canadiana (ebook) 20230206247 | ISBN 9781771339452 (softcover) | ISBN 9781771339469 (EPUB) | ISBN 9781771339476 (PDF)
Subjects: LCGFT: Autobiographical fiction. | LCGFT: Creative nonfiction. | LCGFT: Literature.
Classification: LCC PS8621.A3 B76 2023 | DDC C813/.6—dc23

Printed and bound in Canada

Inanna Publications and Education Inc.
210 Founders College, York University
4700 Keele Street, Toronto, Ontario, Canada M3J 1P3
Telephone: (416) 736-5356 Fax: (416) 736-5765
Email: inanna.publications@inanna.ca   Website: www.inanna.ca

*This book is dedicated to the memory of my brother,
Elliott Joseph Kadar, 1953–2009.*

And to the memory of

*Joyce Penner, 1947–2018
Douglas Freake, 1946–2020
Luciana Ricciutelli, 1958–2020
Ellen Lipes, 1955–2021
Irene Demchuk Parnell, 1941–2022*

CONTENTS

3 Between the Worlds of the Well and the Unwell
5 The Trip
7 Ode to a Node
8 Salvage
11 The Truth
14 Petechia
18 A Work of Art
22 Positively Gin
25 Changing the Subject
28 Soft Figs
29 Her Tears
33 Approaching and Forgetting
36 To Have a Daughter
38 She Made Me Read Sharon Olds and Look What Happened
40 The New Pearl Necklace
44 Alone
47 Regret Powers Love, or, Joseph and Irma
51 Imitation
53 Stairs
56 Three Corners
62 Quietness Is a Poem
64 Ida and Liz
67 My Mother Died?
70 Green Gold, Hard Work
73 My Grandmother Only
75 Fruit Tree They Might Have Planted Before They Were
      Naturalized
76 Defend Me, or, Regret
79 Saving Seats

81 Big Laughing Guy Turns Thirty-One
83 The New Baby and Emma Goldman
87 Remembering, or, Love
88 Another Letter to My Mother
92 Highway 400 Tells Stories about Teens
95 Too Much Beauty
97 The Time Will Come: Part One
100 Christmas Morning 2012
101 Prodigious Peace in Human Metre
104 Injured Sparrow
105 The Time Will Come: Part Two
106 I Heard the Lion Roar
109 Broken Fiction: Part One
110 Dreams
112 Spring Bus Stop
115 Of a Piece – The Conductor
117 Of a Piece, Still The Tall Man
119 When We Are Thirty-Two
120 For Her Twenty-Sixth Birthday
122 He Has a Birthday That We All Play
124 The Voice in the Angle
126 Skin Plus Two Makes
128 For Dori
130 Remembering, or, Disdain
133 The Rabbit Hole
135 To Perform
137 You Have Read This Far from 1320
138 Tears Are Hungarian?
141 One: Turning and Pulling
143 Two: And Then There Is Love
145 Cottage Story, Autumn
147 The Call about My Death

150 Purple Moth
152 So, What Is the Purpose of Our Lives, She Asked
155 It Didn't Start with Me?
163 Cultivating Gullibility

173 *Bibliography*
177 *Acknowledgements*

BETWEEN THE WORLDS OF THE WELL AND THE UNWELL

23 February 2016

When we have lots of money we are able to sustain many illusions about ourselves and others. When we have lots of good health, we can do the same. Those of us fortunate enough to develop addictions in lieu of excessive wealth or death-dealing disease imagine, inspire, relive the illusion of control over one's life for as long as addiction serves the purpose. To whine about the flaws and the faults of the addict: the cost to society of incarceration, hospitalizations, unemployment insurances, and then the most righteous of all, the tragic self-harm the addict performs, can create a kind of nausea, or a headache much like the one Joan Didion describes when she gets a migraine.[1]

The silence and the quiet in which we can do little else but think: striving and martyrdom evaporate; self-punishment persists. But how else can the purity of a conversation take place? A conversation for which a witness has not already entered the scene, agenda intact? As Frank Seeburger says, thinking is a sabbatical practice, the fruit of rest and not of restlessness. It begins only after we are set free to go home to a place not of business but of tranquility, of serenity rather than driven-ness. Seeburger writes:

---

[1] See Didion, 168–72.

> Really to ask a question is to give up the illusion of already knowing the answer, and to give up the sense of control that comes from such an illusion. It is to become, instead, open to learning, ready to be taught—already underway.[2]

I think about this often now, ever since I read the story about the woman who worked in the Canada Kommando at Auschwitz and, years ago, told her version of the "rebellion" gone wrong to a group of Yale historians—among whom sat, thank goodness, a psychoanalyst and survivor himself, Dori Laub. At the time I believe she was sixty-four years old (or maybe sixty-seven): she proclaimed that it was quite the scene when the four chimneys blew up, rubble everywhere, prisoners running, guards shooting. But I, she said, worked in the Canada Kommando, sorting clothes that were meant to be sent on to the guards for their use. Instead, I removed items that prisoners needed and passed them on whenever I could. In other words, the truth that the woman offered the historians was the truth of what it "felt like" to be among others during the explosion, not what it was really "like." The historians dismissed her version of the story as inaccurate. This dismissal is not surprising. Rather it gives us a clue about the fuller meaning of accuracy in the course of storytelling. It provides the lesson we need to figure out how what has become inaccurate out there is just the way life is, and maybe it is our life. Hail Caesar, we are not accurate—neither the survivors who remembered there was only one chimney, or this witness who remembered four.

I have noticed that it is hard for history to give up its control of the story in its restlessness to control the witness.

---

[2] See Seeburger, "Thinking Time, Drinking Time."

THE TRIP

5 November 2016

The zygote contains all the genetic information necessary to form a new individual.

At four weeks, communication erupts into the space between us; I am not an embryo, but I am not insignificant. I can imagine birth and life, but I cannot have it.

On the seventh day,

A female gamete, *1n* haploid cell, runs into a male gamete, *1n* haploid cell; the collision is profoundly simple. But the little moron begins its trip down the fallopian tube without a thought or a map to find a soft and warm home in the lining of her womb. By the fifth day the zygote rests; by its seventh, great works begin.

You don't think it speaks to me, but wind and storm speak in trees. No howling but squishy signs of effort spin into my ears.

A calling like no other, for which no mammal can wield a translation.

Ye of little faith, believe. I am here.

Zygotes collect themselves; the combustion is too grandiose to remain still. I will find my way it says, and you ignore it because it does not exist here. There are no signs yet, just whispers.

ODE TO A NODE

3 February 2016

I have met you before but you weren't as boisterous or portly and
so I had almost forgotten your silhouette.

Now you plague me, a silly little node supposedly full of benign
lymphatic fluids,
a Frankenstein peg in my neck with one to match on the other side.

I can't erase you nor can I hate what you have become since our
first encounter.

Your contours have always been obvious to me, and yet
sometimes loving friends claim not to see you,
you, a swollen lymph node wriggling along a vagus nerve
like a worm.

Lymph nodes never featured in *Vogue,* or even in *Chatelaine*
so I wonder

how you got such genetic credence, so much power over me, so
much stability when I am the one who made you.

SALVAGE[3]

11 December 2017

It never crossed my mind that I was fighting for my life.

The phrase seems overly dramatic.

Typing the letters to write those words hurts my fingertips. This has meant I can't easily speak. I forgot to mention that part when the life-saving chemotherapy began. It is all too trite to complain about, but complain, we do. Poems complain, and so do those we love.

My right hand is bandaged from thumb to mid arm. It looks like the forearm is badly damaged but in fact, it is just punctured. The cotton swaddles, holds in place the infant, an innocuous spike that slips into an injection port that we cannot see until the drip is attached. There is really no pain here. It is the idea that once upon a time a healthy arm turned into a construction site that my body does not feel. All of a sudden, whoosh, my socks hurt my arches, and I wonder.

---

[3] According to the Canadian Cancer Society, "salvage" refers to a chemotherapy or other therapy that is used when blood cancers recur or relapse or are refractory. Thus, the cancer does not respond to the standard treatment or gets worse six months after standard treatment.

The mind does not cooperate with the body during the day, even though the story of pain interests me. The mind knows there is an infant leech sucking the wound. I learned that leeches are brilliant. They release an anticoagulant so that my blood flows effortlessly.

It doesn't always work that way in real life, just in nature. More time, more tries, more wounds, more bandages. Such minor interventions in the scheme of things. That is because my fingertips hurt when I press the keys on the keyboard. I think I mentioned that already: repetition is my strong point. A refrain is our teacher.

I do not want to sound dramatic, but the truth is, living is not a simple matter. Some of us are punctured this way: others, that. A disabled ship is salvaged, or its cargo is retrieved by pirates, and some of us look on. Some of us are on the ship and know that trying to love the subject is theoretical. Like trying to love the subject always is. Consider Katherine [Mansfield][4] or André [Kertész]:[5] why would I love their subjects when I can choose instead to cross the Humber bridge when the sun is shining, or the wind is carrying small waves out to sea? It has been said that my ears won't ring in the breeze. I will hear your voice then and the pain of noise will be stilled.

Across the waves, I heard. "One has left a version of oneself at the place of departure, and it waits for us at the point of return—but she is not me when I get there."[6]

---

[4] See Gunn's *My Katherine Mansfield Project*. This beautiful book was given to me by Paul McHugh at the Faculty of Law, University of Cambridge, who, like Mansfield and Gunn, left his home of New Zealand for new lands.

[5] See Corkin's edited book *André Kertész: A Lifetime of Perception*, especially Plate 58, a shadowy silver print of Boksai Ter, Budapest, 1914. A copy of the image is available at www.mutualart.com/Artwork/Boksai-Ter/1550FB29DAE81DEC.

[6] See the cover of Gunn's book for this quotation.

Against these odds, stealth multiplies. Kind minds swell even when justice seems a mirage. Still, we try. We make laws and courts and train officials who manipulate legal histories and symbols, but only kind minds surface. We resist the fact that justice does not always appear obvious when a tear falls, or my children hold a puppy.

THE TRUTH

21 January 2017

If you get one lymphoma, you get one doctor. If you get two lymphomas, you still get just one doctor. One doctor for two lymphoma is already crowded. In the time it took to diagnose Herpetiformis,[7] all my expectations could have been met. The seas were blustery and the sun, mercurial. There was very little time for me to make a break as the blisters crossed my chest and my scalp, blooming already into large red masses that, although pretty, drove a person mad. A tattoo from left ear to left ankle. I remember that moment on Bloor Street so clearly; so deeply did I notice it that I paused. Yes, I paused on Bloor Street in a beautiful sunshine, near a city trash bin in case my left foot and leg were on a break and could not withstand the sight or the news or maybe the weight of a heart that was screaming: I am ill. Can you hear me? Something is wrong. I have pain that comes out the wrong way. It leaks from under the epidermis until it can quietly make white skin turn purple

---

[7] Dermatitis Herpetiformis (DH) is a chronic condition of the skin associated with and usually accompanied by celiac disease. A strict gluten-free diet is required to avoid complications such as the indolent version of an NHL, non-Hodgkin follicular lymphoma and the aggressive Diffuse large B-cell lymphoma (DLBCL), among other kinds of blood cancers. Sometimes follicular lymphoma transforms into DLBCL, which can be a deadly misadventure, particularly in Hungary and Finland. For more, see Salmi and Hervonen, "Current Concepts of Dermatitis Herpetiformis," and *Celiac Disease Foundation* "Dermatitis Herpetiformis."

and red, as if to say, hey, over there, can't you see me? She is right: this is very painful and now I will make it bleed. Surely someone will notice who has read books or made cue cards. Get the one that says "Skin." Then turn it over. What does it say?

A cue card cannot deliver a diagnosis, I know: I am not that stupid. However, where else do we learn how to catch not a doctor, but a doctor's eyes? A woman in a silky dress who has the panache to grab my ankle. I had only been there a minute, so it was a rather forward act.

Once the ankle was grabbed, though, there was—sadly—no turning back. These eyes were already pure, untainted, ready to hold a foot, to speak purely: you are ill; I will treat you as though you have Leprosy and tomorrow your welts will begin to melt into your inner parts. The process takes time, a lot of time, and you can no longer tease this agony into your skin with sweet, delicious breads. You know, the bread of life.

And Jesus said unto them, I am the bread of life: he that cometh to me shall never hunger; and he that believeth on me shall never thirst. (John 6:35)[8]

And yet hunger and thirst, I did. I went to parties and talked about my research, but it appeared more difficult to speak once the door was closed, to lean against a sofa, then panties abraded my hips and the seams of my jeans burnished my thighs. My hair, innocent hair, like slender metal pins, piercing skin and other material until it is held tightly in place. Why was that needed?

She said, this little white pill will tell us the truth.

---

[8] *The Holy Bible: King James Version*, accessed Mar. 27, 2023, www.kingjamesbibleonline.org/John-6-35/

The Truth Wanders

Philosophers always talk about the truth evolving, that the truth is a wanderer and makes its way in and out of our worlds until it falls into words. Even then, the truth wanders: I know this to be the case. First it was all one way and then, suddenly, it was the other. Warm bread with jam on the canal with Gar and Sue, and *pannekoeken* in the Vondelpark with Sue until there was blood; then rice crackers and chicken livers overlooking the brightly dotted Gardiner Expressway as it competes with parallel cords of traffic like the Lakeshore and the Queensway. Now there is no blood, just tracks in my neck where the jugular had been pierced by a long plastic turkey baster, a slender one that had two similar doors, but each for its own vital function: an in-door, come on in little blood, I won't hurt you; and an out-door, now go out little blood, half dressed. That is right, just half her clothes on because she had the audacity to leave her precious stem cells behind. Right now, those stem cells are who knows where.

But we saw those nurses paddle the thick plastic pouches in which those stem cells lay down, no clue what would happen to them next. A gentle nurse would hold the pouches between her hands, caress them as if they were warm when she knew full well she would press them into a freezer just in case the smelling salts worked and she would wake up to a warm body, a lover whose caress wakened the senses. This is the definition of wandering: cells move.

Cells Move

I walked into the classroom and the words fell out until I could no longer appreciate healthy skin in front of me. I took the bus home, cringing. When I opened the front door I was glad to find a stairway in my view. I sat on the bottom step and held the banister. I could weep.

PETECHIA

22 November 2017

I don't really think about how weird this is: feeling well enough to walk for an hour and yet if I don't get immediate care, I will die in six months.

I don't really feel sad or even anxious. The reason is: I still find this cellular invasion so fascinating. I am curious about its decisions and its pathways, and I am clear that we are not in a battle, but in a symbiosis. If I entertain you and your family, can't you entertain mine, I ask.

When the first infusion of toxic chemicals was fastened to my sore veins, I felt nothing sinister. I was perhaps annoyed by the request for my attention once again. "Multiply relapsed/refractory non-Hodgkin's lymphoma" is such a mouthful: I would prefer something easier to pronounce, something with fewer syllables and no "p's".

But there is one thing I like about the name of the genus of my body's guests. The word, *cancer*, does not appear in most reports; oncologists do not use the word, *cancer*, when they talk about my cells. Sadly, friends and acquaintances are impatient with the measure of syllables—understandably, right?—and resort to "blood cancers," or so I have heard. I want to hear soft syllables. I like the "o's"; I feel the roundness in my wide brow and around my lips. I like knowing that there is a mystery here and that human beings must succumb. Cisplatin and Gemcitabine are like automobiles to me, new automobiles, of course. These are all the wonders of the human mind and sometimes the human heart and they can't help but have their own design. The brilliance of science is tipped for me: I know there is a way that my treatment respects the mystery. It makes no promises, but it makes the effort to promise and promise and promise once again. If our children made the effort, what would we say? Maybe something like: well, dear, that is all you can do, isn't it? What more can we ask for?

My children bob like apples in the barrel. They make every effort to love us and yet carry on with elegant reserve, passionate acceptance, careful loving kindness that is already a part of who they are anyways. They shimmy this way and that, trying out new methods of devotion. They act out pride in their mother and father. They simulate self-possession and sometimes they have the real thing. They weep when I am not looking and smile when I am. They are like pillars by the lake where water and breeze rustle leaves, but gently, quietly, and only the birds will tell us what it is like.

* * *

When I woke up today I brushed my teeth in front of the mirror. And there they were again: the red spots on my chest. The test is: when you press on them, and they don't turn white, they are a sign of thrombocytopenia—the state of too low a level of platelets. Those cells that protect us from bleeding and which I have lost before even when I did not have lymphoma. I bled for hours into a toilet from my nose and then my little girl saved me by calling on our beloved neighbour. Maybe those platelets never did come back home in a real way. Maybe they skipped out onto the dock where fish jump and waves climb onto the shore, but softly.

The donor's platelets were warm and pink, a hue spreading over the flat bag. It did not cross my mind that the donor could be nearby, maybe in the next pod of the chemo daycare wing of the hospital, or maybe down the road in a quieter spot. My donor's blood type is A rh+ and mine is B rh+. I guess they go together but I never knew this. As soon as chemotherapy is over, I am prepped for platelets and they are delivered at the exact right moment. Before delivery, my blood type is confirmed by yet another blood test.

I do not notice anything different when the platelets are transfused; I feel only a bland kind of gratefulness, weary after six hours in the chair already. The transfusion takes one hour and fifteen minutes and then it is all unhooked so that my veins can be flushed with saline. During the flushing, my nurse delivers the sixth injection of Neupogen so that I can stimulate the manufacture of white blood cells—lift the number from .2 to at least 1, as I recall. My tummy is dotted with small bruises: will there be another bruise today when my beloved gives me the injection? He is so skilled, maybe not: I remove the cooler bag from the fridge where the vials of Neupogen rest on top of the lettuce containers. One vial will warm now and soon it will be only a memory.

* * *

Such a beautiful word, petechia. It could be the name of a flower, but it is only the name of a stigmata, a red patch on the skin. The hospital protocol recommends notifying your physician when they appear. They don't mean much to me.

My stigmata are not wholly petechiae. If you look at my torso in the mirror, you can see the shape of the stars in the bruises on my tummy; you can also see the scar just below them, the scar that covers the excision out of which came my first perfect baby. The map is crowned with beautiful purple petechiae, a few above my left breast, one under the arm. Five tiny India Ink tattoos guide the strong arm of the radiation machine while I listen to LCD Soundsystem's "New York I Love You but You're Bringing me Down." A map of irritations mixed in with a bit of pain and a lot of joy. Writers talk about the pain of permanent reminders of cancer, but I like my scars and my tattoos: the joy of courting the body that is doing its best. The malignant cells are not separate from me: they are me. How can I ignore them or despise them?[9]

The next part of this treatment event revs up again in two days, but the petechia may not hold me up. My platelets have not risen despite a transfusion. They still have a couple of days: everyone pray that I can have the "big guns" on Tuesday. That I can welcome back the agony of severe nausea and constant migraine, the inability to drink water, the fear that I have lost my character, my personality, that it has gone to Bar Raval for a martini.

In the middle of the night I woke up to feel my body under our winter duvet—so warm it was I felt as if sunshine was caressing me even though no light appeared in the darkness of near-dawn. That moment remains with me and makes me happy. That happiness is vibrant and perky so I know it is real. There is no reason to feel sorry for me now: I have learned that getting really sick, as I have done recently, leaves only one option—death. If I need to die to avoid that incessant pain and bone-deep nausea and fatigue, then it will be easy to make the transition, I think. Making the transition is my forte in other circumstances, so why not here, too? It doesn't make me sad: I think of it as relief. Relief for my beloved family and friends, too, because they can't all work for me like this forever. It is too hard, too sad for them. And yet it is for them that I agreed to this salvage chemotherapy. It is for them I will manage transplant. It is for them, I will test the waters and the odds.

---

[9] See Amy Gottlieb's article in *The Globe and Mail* that declares a similar sense in its title and elsewhere: "Cancer changed me, but I'm still the same person."

A WORK OF ART

Those are my words not yours

6 August 2018

When the sun came up today, I was listening to the radio, *Ideas* on CBC. How to remake your world when people die. I drifted back to sleep once I had enjoyed the sliver of light that stretched across the blonde floor. I stretched, too, feeling the joy of it all: my legs and feet, stretching, so quietly on the outside but so loud on the inside. Sweet sounds of muscles waking up, meeting sunshine. Pure white percale sliding along my hips. The bed is a work of art, I thought. I have a white bed, and the sheets are ironed and smell of lavender oil. I just go *shake, shake*, and a nub of oil sinks into the pillows.

I didn't know I could stretch my muscles again until I tried it. But that is a scary thing to try when you say, I didn't know I could do it without the sinews splitting or screaming. I walked along the band of light on the floor, marvelling again. Touching cold floor, enjoying the temperature and the firm reception.

I didn't have much to say about this at the time, but now I think: well, now, how miraculous is my body; how tolerant, my feet; how persevering, my muscles. How white my bed. I must have a picture of it in case someone else wants to see it.

A pristinely made bed with white pillowcases and white sheets, which are tucked expertly beneath the mattress.

No twitching, no pain, no spasms.

***

I don't usually find it easy to imagine past brave deeds unless they belong to someone other than me. I think this is a very funny point of departure because bravery is like a stretch. It belongs to all of us in its way and yet, without a context, brave deeds can seem paltry.

Here is an example. I know one woman who, after living in the region for seventy years, she died. She lived in a small condominium that her generous brother had bought for her only a few weeks before. She had been used to living in her minivan, a Dodge Caravan in good condition, but winter was coming and it wasn't clear she would be safe if she didn't drive south again. Which is what she did earlier this year, but we think she felt tired all of a sudden and wanted to stay in one place now that she was a few days from her seventy-first birthday.

The inside of a van through the opened back doors. The backseats have been removed and are replaced with a bare, red twin mattress.

She may have been sleeping peacefully in her new bedroom and just took a last breath; or she may have had a heart attack or a stroke, all alone. She may have been treated unfairly by someone, but how do we know? One thing is for sure: she went to visit my mother in her no-frills seniors' residence. She had time for my mother; I believe she often chatted with elderly women for the pleasure of it.

Out of the blue, she said this: my ultimate homelessness was caused by that eviction... So, one of the guys leading this fight is filming me in my van, etcetera.

I do remember she was evicted, but the story was not transparent. I did not know about the filming.

Months later, we agreed to meet on a Saturday afternoon. She emailed me a few hours before our visit—which meant she wrote to me in the morning, as the sun came up. She typed a message in the subject line of the email so I didn't have to bother opening the message. It said:

> *Hi, Sorry it didn't work out...I think now that I'm out of the van, the last yr is catching up w/me...this A.M. after doing 2 things, I had to go back to bed...maybe when U get bk from East...enjoy the journey & respite.*

Catching up with her. We have all used this expression to say something that strikes us later, or when we yawn more than usual. I thought, this is a delayed response to a physical reality that likely required bravery. Brave deeds every day of her life living on the edge of a home but never really *in* one until that day, that week, so recently, and for such a short time.

POSITIVELY GIN

14 August 2019

I have to admit, I was poised for an encounter, so to speak. Sometimes I forget that I host a nasty little quisling on the inside of my peritoneum, that vague cavity that wraps a clean stomach and a blemished spleen. She goes by the name, Q.

Q's voice can be muffled, but nonetheless evocative. I play audience for a particular woman in the chemo daycare chair who beckons Q: come out quisling, come out and get me, she gestures. On second thought, the cancer-filled woman may have invited Q and I am just being polite in my recounting of the events.

Her black slacks were pressed in *that* way, you know; and she wore well-made strappy black sandals with sexy heels. I can't remember her bodice—quite unlike me, really, not to remember a bodice. I looked for renegade hairs that were sticking out of the chin or the scalp, or a poorly combed part that was lazy, but could find nothing of the sort. That really pissed me off.

By now the lines had been drawn. She was vainglorious; I was woolly-headed. She was graceful; I was awkward. She spoke in a clear and confident voice. She was trying to be *omg I can hardly say it* positive; I was trying to be wayward. Stop it, I said, don't come out, Q. Your value is ill-defined. Your demeanour, off-putting. But I failed and Q had a field day.

Q said, *how are you*, knowing full well that the subject in the chair would be so normal it would piss her off even more.

She said, *great, thanks, how are you?*

Fine, I said—or was it Q that time?

She said, *I have had a fifteen month break from chemo, but I have to start again now.* She was smiling a lot and her voice bounced with a stupid lilt of cheeriness.

Oh, I said, that must be disappointing.

Of course, she said, *but then I am so grateful to get the chemo when I really need it.*

At this point, I knew that my ears were red. I also knew she was going to say that imperative sentence that makes me puke with fury, and she did.

Just stay positive, you have to always have hope. It is incurable, but as long as I can manage it, I am happy to be alive. One day at a time.

I said, I prefer being negative; it is fun, too, ha ha.

At this point, Q was putting on a Superman mask and preparing a large shaker of gin martini with olives and a few blueberries for colour.

***

I had to remember.

My mother would have been ninety-one today.

CHANGING THE SUBJECT

7 December 2016

When I get the results of scans and x-rays, blood work and biopsies, as I did this week, I immediately get confused about what story I must tell to all those sweet interlocutors who keep track of my visits to the hospitals and who ask (with love), well, what happened?

The reason I get confused about what story I must tell has to do with what story they prefer. It is not that they want me to be sick, but neither do they want to hear a story about not-remission. And yet here I feel such enormous pressure to conform to an expectation I barely recognize outside of published academic prose circa 1963 (Michel Foucault's *The Birth of the Clinic: An Archaeology of Medical Perception,* to take one example)[10] that instead of feeling comfort, I feel an unending responsibility to do as the "other" clinic—let's call it the public one that strives in a world of not-cancer—requires: "let's be positive, now," or, "be optimistic." Sometimes very scared people say that optimism keeps cancer patients alive but of course this is a silly claim. This claim hurts the most because it must mean that my friends who have suffered and

---

[10] Foucault can only change the subject because the idea of subjectivity is tied to and re-produced by knowledge and power and their dividing practices. For example, medicine divides the well from the sick, although Foucault would likely prefer the example that psychiatry divides the mad from the sane.

died from cancer or from the inevitable conclusion that eventually chemotherapy runs its course are deficient first, and dead, second. In fact, when I hear this claim about optimism's furious strength, something physical happens inside me, close to the painless scars from the large tumor. I feel unwell immediately, and I fear I might have a reaction that is impolite.

As a former member of the public clinic, I, too, remember a never-ending social desire to neutralize the cancer story. The social clinic desires a story that fits with other illness stories, or at least with the majority of them. Majority is a key word here because there are experiences of illness that belie the assumption about malignant cells: is it the history of malignancy that drives the social wedge between itself and the unwell? Does malignancy trump other death dealing disease in the public's eye, diseases such as ALS disease, depression or MS or Parkinson's?

Mind you, caution always requires pause and pause lurks, even skulks. I skulk. I agree that using the words "pain" and "disease" in the same clause is not wise because the two events do not always go together, or, treatment might be administered allowing a patient with a systemic cancer, like lymphoma, to "feel better." Then what do we do with pain and disease? Of course, I admit, feeling better is a wonderful thing and as soon as it appears I forget that there was an opposite trajectory. Feeling better is a miracle at some junctures in incurable disease. But then there is this: feeling better produces so many new endorphins that it may well also mask the unalterable fact that the subject still has a dangerous underlying disease. But that wasn't well said—of course it masks the fact. Still, isn't the masking a liberation of unparalleled joy? What could be better than living as if five years of illness, treatment, and loneliness had not changed my life forever?

In my own case, relatively good wellbeing hides the *fact* of follicular lymphoma, an incurable but slow growing blood cancer that has invaded every single lymph node in my body and has sometimes slipped on to organs like the spleen and the liver and crawled into the bone marrow. Follicular lymphoma is a shifty character is all we can say. We know that when it starts it is so lazy it may evade detection. We also know that its cells are, at first, small, manageable. As it relapses, it makes bigger cells. Bigger cells are the demise of the cancer that wants to be a chronic disease.

There is yet another, even more threatening danger that hides in its proclivities. Every year follicular lymphoma lives in the body—this it can do as long as the body is protected to a certain level with poisonous treatments—the patient has an increased risk of its shifty character taking hold. It can transform in a heartbeat into a deadly, fast-growing lymphoma, such as aggressive B-cell. In other words, feeling better, as important as it is, is sometimes a poor indicator of the status of the disease. Or maybe systemic blood cancers are just lurkers, and they lurk around. Lurking isn't so bad, really: it is very interesting; it makes me curious. Skulking appears to be of a different order that I am strong enough to usurp, despite my realistic attitude.

But I am losing your attention, I can tell. I may just not have written this up well enough, but another matter may have influenced our rapport. When you are literally outside the circle of the "cancered" you may actually "feel" outside the circle, or even eventually disinterested, tempted to say critical things like "can't you talk about something else already?" or, one I have heard screamed at me a few times this fall, "I had cancer, too, you know." Could optimism have protected me from my impure thoughts? I prefer to keep quiet, you know, and this here is the reason. I am completely curious about lymphoma, but I am not immune to irritations that have nothing to do with being sick. The time has come, mind you. Let's change the subject, shall we?

SOFT FIGS

Dr. Havez from Panama Presiding

7 October 2015

Every visit to a cancer hospital brings both relief and sorrow because no matter what the actual result, it hurts to wait, and it hurts not to wait, because waiting means you live and not waiting means you don't have to wait any more.

After a visit, invasive or not, you want to stop thinking, you want a gigolo, a chauffeur, a latte, soft figs.

Your children seem far away, as if it doesn't matter, and you realize time passes either way. You want to hold hands.

Loved ones still have jobs they think are important. They ask questions but maybe a latte would work.

Well, malignant cells proliferate anyway, and we just want a break. A poem. A meal someone else cooked. Not more news about this or that defect. Not another symptom now.

HER TEARS

6 May 2018

I was forced to sit in an ill-fitting wheelchair because there were neither chairs nor beds nor were there doctors to attend to me or the other forty persons waiting around patiently. Some of us were less patient than others. While I was in that chair—in the middle of a crowded emergency room—a nurse withdrew five vials of my blood. She said: there are no beds.

A very young woman sat across from me in a narrow hallway; she, too, was in a wheelchair. She was speaking loudly. She had been shoeless for some time, I guess. The bottoms of her feet were a dark gray colour. She was very thin and very tired. She may have been nineteen years old.

Another woman, closer to middle age, was also waiting to see a doctor. She carried a white paper bag and she had mostly purple hair. She was also very slender, dressed in black leggings and an attractive sleeveless T-shirt. She was also wearing black and white plastic sandals that were too big for her, so her stride was nothing short of noisy. Her name was Melissa and she appeared to take over social relations in the waiting room of the Emergency Department at Toronto Western Hospital. These relations included attending to the nineteen-year-old who by this time was writhing in her wheelchair and yelling: I am cold. Melissa rushed over with a yellow blanket that she took from an ambulance driver. Soon after, another young woman dressed in black was wheeled into the waiting room; she was screaming and yelling at the two female paramedics who were holding her up. Some women control care; others beg for it.

Into the noise was wheeled another young woman; she was white and healthy. In her lap were two sloppily bandaged wrists and hands, and a bicycle helmet. I could not find my breath so I did not speak even though her wheelchair was touching mine. Then I realized that this young woman could have been my own girl, my daughter riding a bike along the tracks on Davenport. Melissa did not tend to this young woman. I figured she was there to care for a group of young women longing to find a heartbeat, a bathtub filled with warm water and vibrant essential oils. Maybe eucalyptus or lavender. She returned with Tim Horton's Honey Cruller doughnuts. She gave one to her friend who was very grateful.

The young woman in the wheelchair next to me had a northern European name—maybe it was Dutch, or maybe even Irish. She had red hair. Sitting still and silently all this time, she finally got my attention. Taking a deep breath, I turned and asked: did you have a bicycle accident?

She said: yes, barely moving her head.

I said: are you in pain?

She said: yes, oh yes. She spoke quietly. Her face was so still that I wished I could hold her.

I said: can you ask for some pain medicine, but she indicated she had already been given some.

I then said: where did you have the accident?

She explained: on the train tracks up near Davenport; do you know where I mean?

I said: yes. I am sorry.

A moment passed and her face drooped in sadness. She did not seem to notice Melissa or her wards, but that is what pain does to you, isn't it? You don't see when pain calls out and creases the skin under the eyes.

(Melissa walked quickly with confidence across the waiting room, rushing as if she knew where she was going. When her name was finally called, Melissa was outside on the lawn smoking a cigarette.)

I said: do you have someone you can call to be with you here?

(It is hard to wait alone when your arms hurt and your hands curl, or you can't find your breath because your sternum is tight.)

She said she was writing to someone now, but I could see her hands didn't work very well.

I said: are your parents near?

That was the moment that stung and tears came down. My tears came down, too, as I thought about Emma and her bike accident in Montreal, far away from a parent. Far from our home together. The Dutch or Irish woman wept so I took some tissue out of my bag. I motioned to her to take one but she said, I can't lift my arms.

I said: oh darling, do you want me to wipe your tears for you and she said, yes.

I wiped the tears gently from her cheeks. Then I wiped my own tears away with a clean tissue, imagining my young family, rejoicing in memories of the children I have loved.

She said: thank you.

APPROACHING AND FORGETTING

Mother's Day 2019

The oncologist was, as often happens in the world of a cancer hospital, late. I waited at the north end of the building, but sometimes I was instructed in the portal to wait in the south end. Both ends had boring waiting rooms with televisions repeating the same old news; both waiting rooms kept patients rather comfortably between arriving at their destination, and yet not fully disembarking.

When I turned my head, I noticed the oncologist at my desk. He was opening drawers and rummaging around the papers that had been carefully assembled as if with good reason—though, predictably, out of order. For some banal reason, the papers always look so neat, so clean and uniform, but they never make the sense you had hoped they could do.

I watched the oncologist from the portal, but he did not notice me. He was wearing a yellow, paper-thin cape to protect him from my germs. I spoke his name, but then a blank, an empty silence, a quiet room. How often does this happen, I wondered. Could I have made a mistake here? Was it really my oncologist, or was I abroad somewhere, unable to approach?

There was only one thing left to do. I decided to call my mom for a lift because she always said "yes." Her voice made me happy. I could see half of her bodice in my mind's eye because my father had ripped a photo in half and bequeathed the left side of the image to me. My half-mom was wearing the silky red and white skirt and blouse ensemble fashioned by *Bay Club*, perhaps in 1988, size twelve. It was *Made in Canada*. If you look closely, you can see the pattern of bird-like shapes repeated with precision; and you can see my mother's beautiful hands. Sadly, her face is missing. I wonder now what my father saw on the other side of her face, why he tore it like that, the photograph, roughly.

A photograph that has been torn raggedly down the middle, splitting the image of an older woman dressed in a smart blazer over a red and white silk blouse in half.

There was a time when my mom could be seen wearing the whole outfit, complete from top to bottom, left to right. Because I fancied seeing my mother as my own, I stole the skirt and blouse when she could no longer see the gowns hanging in her closet. Nor could she see her own daughter then because her eyes had stopped working just like that, overnight, in one second, lights dimmed.

A silken, patterned red and white blouse with matching skirt laid one on top of the other on an oak hardwood floor.

I ran to the car and forgot about a familiar looking doctor sorting through my things. There is no greater joy than forgetting about a doctor, let me tell you.

TO HAVE A DAUGHTER

2015?

Those many times when young women think they can bake a cake
Turned around
And off they have gone which is what they said you wanted
them to do
(and you know what she means)
Does not really capture the context

In which things said protect.

Those many times when young women think that mothers
humoured will be quiet,
Keep love contained, free her for other loves.
Turned around
And every message as if Rossetti or Akhmatova
Just like she said it would be, far away,
not seeing the streets she walks along,
The shops she passes or the beer and urine cocktail she smells when
the sun bakes the sidewalks.
Cannot really capture the context

By the time you hear her voice again
She is twenty-eight years old and living in Brooklyn
Turned around, oh great joy.

SHE MADE ME READ SHARON OLDS AND LOOK WHAT HAPPENED

20 March 2019

There was a time when separating from you actually made the house shake. I washed your clothes and hung them without pegs to dry on a rack outdoors, the way you do when you love to watch your laundry billow. Mind you, sometimes laundry will fall to the damp ground so that you have to run out and say, oh no, her white blouse will be green-smudged. I will pick it up and pretend it is just such a nuisance to take care of fabric, isn't it?

Sometimes I would shake when she left, and I always had to hold back my tears until they flooded, sometimes before she actually stopped looking. Her childhood seems so brief now. I know I will see her in my dreams, and maybe we will cook together. She might go out in the evening but I will leave my door open so I can hear her when she tip-toes back up the stairs, maybe too late, maybe confused, maybe alone. Isn't it funny the chinks we see now in our love? There must be a prayer that can be repeated, the rosary maybe, so that it feels less laden, less beset.

Her slender legs slide alongside my mother's legs on the bed. The door to her room is ajar. She holds my mother's limp hand in hers, and in her other hand, she holds a pink phone. Her body mimics the shape of my mother's body as they curve around each other. I have to think about my words here because one of them really is very slender and the other, just thin—no other way to say it. One of them has smooth skin—we would all say that; the other, folds of bluish skin, still handsome in its way.

At some point there appears to be a heat exchange and my mother's lips turn pink again; she may be asleep, I think, blind eyes closed, shapely forehead like a roof over a closed window. Oh, my, I realize I have never seen my mother without glasses. The widow's peak the same, I mumble, some things never change. Others change readily.

That house is gone now, and so is my mother, and my girl, she is away. We will cook together tomorrow and have a Sunday dinner the way we have always done. If she needs to leave early, I will wrap my slender body around the curves my mother has left in the mattress. I will take off her glasses before she falls asleep again. Her dying seems so brief now, and yet still so near, so loved.

THE NEW PEARL NECKLACE

2 April 2018

She had been trying to write a story about a pearl necklace. But it wasn't working. She got stuck on Steinbeck's rewriting of the parable, *The Pearl*, a story that did not end the way she had wanted it to. So she changed it.

It went like this.

***

There had been a gift of pearls. The gift was from the mother to the daughter on a momentous occasion. At the time the daughter didn't know how to wear pearls. It is possible she had not been properly groomed.

Then there was my own mother.

She last wore her pearls eight years ago: as always, she is beautiful in pearls. Her smile tells a dreamy story. Look here at this portrait: can you see what I mean?

An older woman, with cropped hair pulled back off her face, smiling broadly, sporting wire-rimmed glasses, large-beaded earrings and a pearl necklace.

I know. I know. The pearls are fetching on an LBD.[11] There is a sense of order in the arrangement, and a coupon that marks some kind of entry. As Jackie Kennedy said, "pearls are always appropriate."

Okay, fine: but it is the smile that I hold now. I am pretty sure it says, yes, you love me, and I love you. How can we celebrate this here and now if you are gone?

I forever ask this question and think: the answer is the gift of pearls.

---

[11] Little Black Dress.

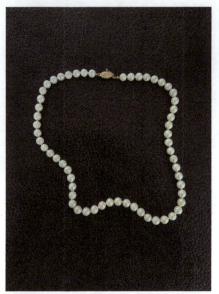

A white pearl necklace with a golden clasp laid out on a backdrop of black leather.

I recall I opened a brown velvet box lined with silk. We were all in a restaurant that used to be on Bay Street, probably the *Csárda*.[12]

The velvet box gave it all away. *Oh, Mom, you bought pearls for me.* I immediately felt I had crossed over even though it is still possible I hadn't been properly groomed for that particular moment. I thought of my mother's Hollywood heroes—Audrey Hepburn and Grace Kelly, Sophia Loren and Bette Davis. They all wore pearls with an LBD and looked almost as glamorous as my mother. It was a thing, and it signified a style and a fashion where my mother and I hid, holding hands.

---

[12] *Csárda* is the Hungarian word for an inn, a summerhouse, a tavern.

✳ ✳ ✳

The story might work now. It is a dream that others have glorified. But only my mother is the hero of this one.

A rectangular, black velvet box sitting on top of a writing desk.

ALONE

23 January 2020

I gave her a short, fat, Mead Five Star notebook. She wrote her grocery list in it, but it wasn't easy to make the letters anymore. Some letters made words that I cannot now decipher, but maybe you will find the meaning that I can't find.

carrots
Celery G. pepper
onions
Tomatoes
lttuce
fruit
ice cream
Butter
 scrub it
 Hermant
Bleach
paper towels
Kraft
Balsamic
garlic onion

Two c words in that list: almost alliteration, I thought. It would be so much better if she could phone the store herself. Mind you, it was just easier to take the list and make the call myself—it was such a little thing and I was happy to do it, really.

I said once: are you lonely? She said she wasn't which gave me some relief.

The next time I asked for the shopping list, it went like this. There was no alliteration, but there was a shape to the way the items were collated.

garbage bags
Quisants
Tomato Juice + orange
Chicken- weiners
Fruit
ice cream
tomatoes small
Balsamic. Salt
potato Chips
Balsamic dressing

She couldn't see the words on the page, she said, and she then paused and whispered: I am lonely.

I turned the page. Just one word on the top of an otherwise empty page. She had written: Diplomat. Again, I had no idea what this meant, if anything. All I can see now is the sadness between the words, the intensity in the silhouette of the lists, the loneliness.

I now feel so lonely without her, without that innocent sweet woman who called me darling at every opportunity. I know that she was thanking me for calling the police. Not this time, but the first time when my father hit her with a coat hanger.

I saw red.

I thought: if I love them both equally, I can save my mother. I am not sure how that would work in real time, but in a kid's head, it seemed a spot-on observation with do-able outcomes.

What is a Diplomat, I wanted to ask? The answer is clear now, but it might be too late for a solution. A Diplomat is a go-between, someone who makes deals that appear to smooth over the wrinkles, the heartache, the sobbing.

When I turned the crumpled page, I touched something fibrous. It was a passport photograph of her father. This photo was taken at Kennedy Travel on Queen Street at the corner where my grandfather shuffled through the Future Bakery garage for light rye bread and MC dry cottage cheese.

By now you realize that the travel "agency" was an oasis where we met other interlopers who anticipated special treatment.

"Speak Slovak and make it all work for me, please."

A musical refrain that could be repeated in semitones, or in the bizarre intervals between the notes of octaves that Doug would sprinkle over the martinis.

Doug preferred Liszt.[13]

---

[13] Douglas Freake is a brilliant musician who taught me about octaves.

REGRET POWERS LOVE, OR, JOSEPH AND IRMA

7 April 2020

Irma Rombauer[14] starts *The Joy of Cooking* with a question: "did you know that baked beans are as traditional in Sweden as they are in Boston?" They are apparently served on Shrove Tuesday in Swedish homes. The last festive food before Lent, they say. What shall I give up for Lent, I wondered, and knew that Lent was likely a foreign idea to Irma.

Irma's half-brother, Max Starkloff, was the inventive Health Commissioner who introduced the idea of "social distancing" during the 1918 Spanish Flu pandemic.[15] Irma's husband, Edgar, killed himself in 1930, so she had to write a cookbook to put food on the table.

The recipe is the connection here: let's cook up some poor man's meat, she said. White navy beans seem so perfectly shaped, so similar in size and colour. The recipe is plain. The beans need to stew in a slow oven for six to nine hours.

---

[14] Irma S. Rombauer and Marion Rombauer Becker, *The Joy of Cooking*, Toronto: Thomas Allen and Son, 1931; rpt. 1972.

[15] Starkloff instituted gathering bans and closure orders in St. Louis that sound much like those we are familiar with today. St. Louis suffered fewer deaths from the flu than other American cities as a result. See *The American Influenza Epidemic of 1918–1919: A Digital Encyclopedia*. "St. Louis, Missouri."

Do this, do that. The recipe is cushioned by instructions that are near poetic. Rombauer says, decorate the beans with salt pork. Which of course I would never do. I decorate with carrots that are getting old and brown. Just peel them, I said.

It wasn't my idea to use carrots for decoration. It was his idea, these carrots. To the right of the list of ingredients are perfectly shaped letters, words that Joseph had made into simple addenda. Nobody thinks that their cookbook addenda might be preserved forever when they first write them. I think of recipes from the camps that didn't work out when I think of addenda. This recipe must work, I thought, or he would not have messed up the typescript with a medium blue fountain pen.

It was also his idea to add yeast extract, often used by hippie-cooks in those days. The book was copyrighted in 1931, hard times in 1931. My version of the fat white book was likely printed in 1972, the year I hooked up with Joseph. By then, Rombauer had died, but I didn't take notice. Now I notice because that marriage died and it was all my doing. The book is tattered.

A very old cookbook with fraying edges and the hardcover held together by tape.
The dustjacket is missing, revealing a white hardback with "Joy of Cook" emblazoned on it.

I consulted my new gods, asking if I could send an apology to Joseph, perhaps on the back of the recipe. He would read it with his newer French-speaking Flemish wife at his side, and they would say, oh that is so nice that she apologised. Joseph would add, I feel so much better now. He would then write me a letter in medium blue ink, a fountain pen, yes, and thank me for thinking of him. Maybe one day we can meet again, he might gesture. I guess *I* would feel so much better at that point. I might start knitting again, the rusty orange wool that I bought on the east coast. The colour of lobster shell, the vendor said. I invented this colour, she said—a shade on this side of orange and that side of the rusty planks in the harbour.

Joseph was born in Utrecht, not so far from Brussels really. The Dutch make fun of the Belgians and the way they cook and eat *frites*. Cultures too close for comfort, I guess—and a complicated border. One foot here and one foot there. When things are this close, who will you blame?

A cobblestoned street marked with a line of white crosses painted into the stone. These crosses mark the border between Belgium and the Netherlands, marked by a "B" and "NL" respectively.
(Credit: Alix Guillard. Licensed under the terms of CC-BY-SA 2.0.)

The borders are marked with white crosses on roads, pavements, and buildings.[16]

Joseph's father-in-law, once a wrestler, immigrated to Alberta as a young man. He made a fortune in Calgary, where he owned an acclaimed strip club. I always wondered about this; his daughter is a warm-hearted elegant woman and, like most women I knew, a feminist who had run away from another husband. She may have been damaged, I thought—but on the other hand, maybe not. How would I know?

Joseph was too good a man not to be damaged. Such a gift, he said: *The Joy of Cooking* is such a gift. Irma's leg was amputated in between her seizures. She may have chosen an early death anyways, but her family wounds are profound. The stuff that fiction is made of. See. I pretend to know. I won't achieve forgiveness this way.

But then, what is there to forgive? Regret belongs to us. It punctuates the recipe as bleakly as it circles our life. It reminds us that it is actually Goethe who opens *The Joy of Cooking*.

That which thy fathers have bequeathed to thee, earn it anew if thou wouldst possess it.[17]

There is no tradition of baked beans or proper *frites*. There is only all the effort in between the moments of greatest declarations, and the trying to forget or remember all at once in a fury of somersaulting regret.

---

[16] "Elections split Dutch-Belgian community." BBC News, 2009. The article explains: "the international border that separates the Belgian town of Baarle-Hertog from the Dutch town of Baarle-Nassau does not run straight. It is not even curved."

[17] The line is from Johann Wolfgang von Goethe's *Faust*, The First Part, 682–83.

IMITATION

15 October 2020

The voice of books informs not all alike.[18]

I read the *Imitation of Christ*[19]—written between 1418 and 1427—when I was nineteen years old, summer of 1969. The book was lovely to handle: it was protected by a matte blue cover that felt like velvet, and the pages were thick cotton-like. My copy of the book is small. The problem is: I can't find my copy of the book, which puts me at a disadvantage. I am not able to guess how many pages it is. I have to trust you to believe me.

I prefer to call the book by its original title: *Imitatio Christi*. Maybe you think this is pretentious, but sounds make me feel reverent, and the sound of Latin takes me quite close to the altar. I genuflect, of course, and I make the sign of the cross on my body. These gestures are automatic because I feel no thought. They are stitched in as memory, a wholesome memory-trace in which we sit and wait for

---

[18] My first reflection on this line comes from the third edition of Jonathan Rose's *The Intellectual Life of the British Working Classes*, p. 13.

[19] See Kempis.

a gem to emerge or a shadow to engage our curiosity.[20] The gem and the shadow, they are of a piece, never certain and certainly consistent only in how often they change themselves.

The *Imitation of Christ* reminds me of my first holy communion in 1965 and my first wedding which took place in a Roman Catholic church in 1972. I thought then that my wedding was sacred, and so was my marriage. But I must have abandoned that *thought* before it had time to brew up, or thicken, or before I was wise enough to work it out. Many years later I asked: is there no text outside the written one I cherished? The question seems irrelevant now.

My idea was that if I did as Thomas à Kempis asked—assuming it really was Thomas who wrote the book—I would succeed at being a good person, a very good person. Thomas made me feel humble and responsible, just as his subject must have done years before him.[21]

He told me: be not angry that you cannot make others as you wish them to be, since you cannot make yourself as you wish to be. Kempis buttonholed Derrida when he said that "the voice of books is indeed one, but it informs not all alike."[22] I was immersed. Mind you, what he says afterward doesn't really support my theory.

I thought that was a good thought at the time.

---

[20] The idea of the memory-trace is taken from Sigmund Freud's *Beyond the Pleasure Principle*, first published in German in 1920. In the fourth chapter, Freud writes: memory-traces "have nothing to do with the fact of becoming conscious; indeed, they are often most powerful and most enduring when the process which left them behind was one which never entered consciousness."

[21] So did George Eliot—her Maggie Tulliver roamed the Lincolnshire countryside with *Imitation of Christ* in her hand, hoping to discover what could satisfy a Victorian lady whose identity was only obvious to her spiritual heroes. See *The Mill on the Floss*, Chapter 7.

[22] Kempis, p. 188.

STAIRS

24 February 2016

Let's just have a little sit-down here, Mom. Everything will be alright: I can handle this; you are just getting ahead of yourself, worrying about what might happen, not thinking about what actually is happening. What is happening is: I am lounging comfortably a few steps from the attic, thinking about how good I am and how cute you think I am. Not all babies fall down stairs. I am seven months old already—I will be the one who does not fall. You'll see.

And if I just turn my leg this way, and then see what I can do with my hand. Sort of like what you do when you are pretending you are a warrior. I can rest my hand and arm on my knee, like so. I think it helps me to rest when I am really high up like this.

Oh Mom, that's not true. I can take care of myself, just like I do now. I am smiling because I can see you are scared about this silly fall idea, but mom, chill, it is not going to happen today. Let's wait until I can do it on a harder surface, when we can get some blood out of the blast! Here we have this ugly turquoise broadloom under us, a perfect pillow for my sore knee.

I know you are admiring my hairdo because the whole mess is brushed forward as if I was partially bald. I have seen older men do that these days when their hairlines recede. My hair is wispy; the locks are dark; their shape may have been molded by my rather long-lasting birth. Or maybe by the forceps. Do you remember the forceps, Mom? I wasn't sure you were all there when that new doctor marched in and tried them out on my head. Maybe you were tired—but she was just learning. Oh no: did I say something wrong (again?). I know it wasn't your fault; life happens like that and then things change. I can feel a smile coming on just remembering our romance that day, how much you seemed to love my grin, my chuckle, how satisfied it made me to see my mother's joy when all I really wanted was food. How could I forget?

I can't remember if my big sister was still around—I know she saved me up here and then all of you just started staring at me, like you were proud of me and yet terrified at the same time. I have decided this is a look only parents get, and as they get older, they do it more and more often, without reason. I am not saying you weren't reasonable; I am just saying sometimes you behave irrationally around me. Like that day you came to pick me up at school and you couldn't find me? I bet they heard my name in that high octave as far as Buffalo. I won't even bother about when you found the bong in the shed.

A small child, wearing striped, one-piece pajamas and boots, crouches on carpeted stairs, looking backward over their left shoulder, smiling.

THREE CORNERS

8 March 2016

A sepia-toned family photograph, featuring a woman wearing a billowing, floor-length dress standing next to her young child, who is propped up on a table so that they are nearly shoulder-to-shoulder. Michalovce, Slovakia, 1929.

That moment when Baba rolled out the dough on the old wooden pastry table: I love that moment. My grandfather must have put the thing together soon after they had arrived. I think they disembarked in Quebec City. It looks nothing like this table, and my mom would never be allowed to stand on a pastry table, I can assure you.

The pastry table now belongs to me. I don't use it for much. But I continue to marvel at the dip in the surface of the table. The rolling pin against my grandmother's terrifically strong hands and as time passed, under the bare arms striped with razor thin scars. She had ironed a gentle valley into the fibres of the blonde wood. Do you see it?

An heirloom, wooden pastry table with one drawer in the middle.
The tabletop has been worn down into a concave curve from the years of use.

It is a slight scoop, a floured curved, soft and smooth like a baby's cheek, wiped clean for eighty years but never really washed, no no.

Soon after our little hands had been washed with soap (again), my brother and I gathered with Baba on stools in the cold kitchen to pinch perogies. Baba lined up the dough-parcels on the table like little soldiers in a silent marching band until the dip disappeared under their capes.

Perogies, soft dough folded tightly over filling and pinched closed, lined up like soldiers on a pastry table, sprinkled with flour. (Credit: Adobe Stock)

The perogies were later put to sleep, laid on the downstairs bed for a cool nap. Here they dried in an angle of sunlight from the window, three-cornered gluey packages whose soft edges were methodically pinched together—some ended up more isosceles but mine were more precisely equilateral. Flour and water make glue, but you already know that. Yes, the edges of perogies stick together with the edible glue of flour and water, just like the staves of wine barrels in more glorious cold kitchens in the underground caves of Eger or Budapest. I am not dropping names. It is just the way things are: the memory of Eger gives me goosebumps. Eger, from which Toronto's teenaged boomers drank "bull's blood," a raw red wine that cost a few dollars in 1968. Most of us can't imagine now that we would have stooped so low then: after all, a decent extra dry gin martini costs more than two bottles of bull's blood.

We don't think of irony when we think of three corners. My grandfather laughed so hard when his full tummy grumbled after eating a large platter of perogies drenched in browned butter and topped with MC sour cream, only MC. He said: the three corners are fighting in my tummy. Ho ho ho. The three corners really were soldiers, I thought, and wondered why he found this idea so funny, and me, I found it so normal.

Sometimes what we love most as children comes back to hurry us into adults. I guess I did not realize then that Hungarian corners can come apart and raise their fists in preparation for genetic battle. Eating more and more perogies until I felt sick, I could not wait for the next Friday night when we would do the same thing all over again. Maybe overeating perogies was a childish sign I should have read with more mature eyes.

Friday arrives again at last. At three-thirty we three would drive to Mimico from Long Branch and pick up my grandmother at Continental Can in Zedo's pristine slate-gray Hudson. She would emerge minutes after the siren sounded, walking with a waddle and a smile, her hair twisted up in a pastel-coloured cotton kerchief we had ripped into a square so that it could be properly folded to keep the hair safely out of the way of saw-sharp steel panels and other edges. To me, a well-folded kerchief gave my grandmother a crown of majesty. All the other women on the line were equally skilled and folded their headgear in the exact same manner. To me this was the look of beauty: a ribbon of pink, yellow, and blue kerchiefs bobbing up and down the long sidewalk that brought Baba from the steel into my sweet smooth-skinned arms. For forty years she walked that line and never missed a day.

Marcela Bednarik at work at Continental Can, New Toronto, around 1960. She is wearing heavy work gloves, coveralls and a headscarf as she handles a thick sheet of steel metal on the factory line.

Little did we know my arms, too, would become scarred, but I was not heroic like Baba. I did not carry twenty-foot steel panels in the air, avoiding the heads and bodies of fellow workers and bypassing loud machinery. No, no: my skin erupted in a blistering disease with a long name because of those three corners making war under the surface of my skin, screaming at blood corpuscles, and filling up the lymphatic rivers of my body with poison until the bed sheets themselves appeared to breathe, I mean, bleed. Flour and water, they said, make blood flow up like geysers in some countries. Suicidal itch, they said.

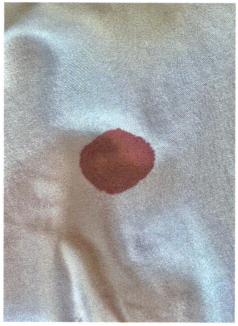

A close-up showing a splotch of bright red blood staining a white, silken fabric.

(Wait: if I eat perogies on a Friday night, are they saying I might die?)

In other countries, nothing like this happens. Life just goes on and little girls eat perogies and wipe the flour out of the dip of the homemade pastry table with joy, without fear. In the morning their skin is the same as it was last night.

QUIETNESS IS A POEM

1 November 2017

Waiting to hear is worse than hearing.

When one hears, one knows; when one waits, one does not know, or at least one pretends one does not know. Neither does one need to see the forest which may have the effect of greening, of protecting the environment when every cell in your body knows that such protection is, apart from self-aggrandizing, also foolish, selfish, or both.

When the waiting ends, it is the fool who feels the superficial pleasure of a make-believe solution. Like solving crimes, I have solved my own impatience with waiting by caressing a baby or juggling a puppy, or kissing my husband's yielding temple, unchanging and tender, lashes parting and lips curving just that little bit, waiting for the warm when it meets warm.

There are few pathways, whether we are talking about the nervous system or the blood, or the route I take when I cycle to my mother's so-called home. I, too, try to say it is her home but every cell in my body tells me there is nothing like our home here or there, that it is just a stop on the pathway where we all pretend home is where the heart is when no such place exists between walls.

There are even fewer ways to measure joy, but the measurement itself is joyous if only because it is active. It has always been the passive nature of my nature that has annoyed me and convinced me to cross over and move my feet, bend my legs, take my arms to the heavens. The curious nature of the eyes and the brain at rest, the hands held across the lap, the feet swaddled on a warm pillow.

We just want it to be quiet now. Just quiet. The grief is a memory, not an act. Quiet; passive; no turns.

Fewer full sentences.

IDA AND LIZ

10 January 2020

Ida knew she was special.

She probably learned this from the inside. Not because she was told by some elder person with good intentions.

She was often described as poised, and wise seeming.

She was only five years old when she held a pencil as if it was a cigarette holder that had been snatched from Elizabeth Taylor's trailer on the set of Joseph L. Mankiewicz's *Cleopatra*.

The photograph was reproduced on Ida's birthday, although she wasn't born until 1984. Surely there is a suggestive or sloping link between Ida and Elizabeth that we could not see until today.

Ida had long slender fingers. Her nails were rose-pink and evenly shaped, just like my mother's. My mother loved Elizabeth Taylor, but also felt sorry for her. My mother smoked Du Maurier cigarettes. They were lined up like pencils in a hot red package. Ida played the piano.

A 1961 *Life Magazine* cover featuring Elizabeth Taylor, smoking a cigarette, celebrating her first Oscar win over a bottle of champagne. (Credit: Entertainment Pictures / Alamy Stock Photo)

My mother was very beautiful. She married a crooner who wooed every woman who approached his space. I had assumed that one day I would be as handsome as my mother, or my father.

I had heard that my parents were the "Hollywood couple." Heard means: in the Slovak and Hungarian clubs, which weren't really clubs but cells of the Party where nobody spoke English.

My parents looked the part of Taylor and Burton, but my father broke my mother's heart. Then I think my mother broke mine; and

my brother, broken-limbed, loved my mother instead. I understand
the deal he made.

My father bought my mother stylish gowns from Starlight Imports
in Dixie Plaza. I especially loved the sky-blue sweater with the gold
lamé scalloped neckline and childlike cap sleeves.

I hold the sweater to my face when my heart aches so much for her
that Ida cries.

MY MOTHER DIED?

9 March 2018

I have been away from the blank page for almost three months now. Facing it again is not so difficult although the number of surprises I can describe makes me think about life as endlessly endless.

When my eyes open I see my mother's beautiful blue eyes staring at me endlessly and wonder why they don't work. How is it that beauty and function do not cooperate? Forcing the issue (my mother would say I always *force* the issue), I tried to fill the gap between what her eyes don't see and what I can see for her. I even rejoined the Slovak church with her and we prayed the rosary together. She stayed in her wheelchair and I cuddled her with my free hand as we shuffled the smooth black beads on my father's rosary, the beads I loved so dearly as an adolescent. The priest came to us, not the other way around.

Can you imagine that my mother died when I was not looking? How could such a thing happen when I needed her the most? I am not sure why I feel bereft because I have continued to pretend that she is still here, just down the street with her friends—Bunny, Antoinette and Parul and the other residents. Laughing, I have heard others call them inmates.

***

My mother belongs to me, not to them, and they have no right to take her from me. I am not going to cry—you must be able to see that now—because I want to be righteous and noble when I think of my mother's love.

Then it all softens. It softens into the truth. I am bereft. My mother has died. I am now alone. And at the same time, I cannot always lift myself off the sofa. When you feel this kind of resistance in the thighs you want your mother to help lift you. You want a mother who can see and feel and think as if she were still the wise one in the family. You want a mother like mine: beautiful, resilient, and always trying to do better.

You want a mother.

I want a mother.

Trying to do better all the time is a curse. Your children will always betray you: they have no choice. I know that and so do you, so don't pretend any more that she is alive.

***

The last time I saw my mother I was swaddled in winter fabrics that ensured my isolation. The room was pink with love. My sweet girl was holding her grandmother's hand and had done so all day long, waiting for me, her mother, to arrive. Pink love swirled in my heart and in hers as we tried to remember this was the end. We knew long ago love was pink and that death would not be the tyrant we find in Romans (5:17) or the thief Jesus has concocted to make us afraid (Matthew 24:42-44) when what we know is not fear, but sorrow and joy, admixed.

There was a soothing in the love we all shared in that room, the love that we could not describe because the surprises were endless, they kept coming, they stretched the swaddles and pierced the space.

I knew my mom was finished when she died because she could have done it any time. She chose to wait for her granddaughter to arrive to hold her hand as she ploughed through the memories and the troughs of sensations that stuck to her gauzy skin. She lay on her side watching in her blind way, perceiving the pink and I pray, the love that filled her room on that memorable weekend. As I said before, your children must always betray you, and so I did. I stood there. I did not cry. My own baby sobbed with the love that has always been hers. "My angel," my mother cried. "My little golden girl," my mother sighed. *Moje zlaté dievča*, my mother remembered as if no time had passed.

GREEN GOLD, HARD WORK

13 July 2020

Seven tobacco harvesters stand atop a wooden wagon, raising the long, green tobacco leaves aloft, smiling, proud of their work.

I have been sorting through thousands of photographs collected primarily by my father. He was an amateur photographer, an amateur violinist, an amateur builder, and a professional salesman.

The images challenge me. They generate so many memories, but then again, so much history that I could never have remembered because it "didn't start with [me]."[23]

The most precious images are of me as a child. Before I was born, my mother and my aunt were very good friends. There are so many photographs of them enjoying life together. Too many for me to accept, so I threw them away. The garbage truck came Friday so I cannot get them back.

Before I was born my mother and my aunt went with my grandmother to Delhi, Ontario, to pick "green gold."[24] It may have been 1948 or 1949. The women were young, maybe nineteen years old. In those days, Delhi farmers hired Canadian immigrants. Delhi, it is said, sounded like Casablanca, many languages were spoken at the same time: mainly, Belgian French or Flemish, and Hungarian.

Terribly sad: the photograph is blurry and the lines are unclear. In the tiniest version, I do see the faces of the women in my life as vibrant and happy, even as they pick tobacco. The tobacco leaves are as long as my mom is tall.

I wonder why they are so separate now even though I have two different views of whose fault it is that they do not speak to each other any longer, that they do not laugh together, cook together, speak broken Hungarian together.

Only a few years later, they coo over the darling baby, and my father takes a photograph that could sink a ship or two. He dressed me up and somehow got me to warm my eyes with the love I felt for my family. I can feel it now, just like the red worsted wool of the sofa on which I am perched.

---

[23] See Mark Wolynn's *It Didn't Start with You.*

[24] See Edward Dunsworth's article "Green Gold, Red Threats: Organization and Resistance in Depression-Era Ontario Tobacco."

A young child with short blonde hair sits on a red-checkered, wool sofa. She is dressed fancily, with a deep red velvet necktie over a plaid waistcoat.

The fabric was manufactured in Norfolk, England, in a town named Worstead. Green Gold was farmed in Norfolk County in Ontario, in a town named in honour of Delhi, India. What can we say about love and complicated grief?

MY GRANDMOTHER ONLY

2012

My grandmother only drank Pride of Arabia 100% arabica coffee in the brown bag from Loblaws 1950–1965 at ninety-three cents a pound.

My grandmother only used Ivory soap. It floated in the tiny Gort Avenue bathtub and that is how we knew it was pure.

My grandmother had machine gun filings in her skin from lucrative wartime work in the munitions factory and the factory doctor said: "use Noxzema on your face, only Noxzema."

She was one of forty thousand women who made bombs for B52s and Sten guns.[25]

Now you are getting it.

My grandmother only used Noxzema skin cream on her face.

---

[25] The Sten Gun was first used by Canadian troops on the Dieppe Raid, August 19, 1942, built in Canada mostly by women. The gun was not popular among soldiers; it jammed often and went off by accident. They called it the "Plumber's Nightmare" and sometimes the "Plumber's Abortion" because it was ugly. See the entry "Sten Gun," on the *Canadian Soldier* website for more.

After the war my grandmother wrapped her hair in pastel-coloured kerchiefs.

Each afternoon, we picked her up at the steel factory in a grey Hudson at three-thirty, when the shift bell howled. We were never late.

Then she unwrapped her hair as we drove to J. I. Case Company on Vickers Road where we were the janitors.

We ate supper in my grandfather's cozy office, the boiler room, and then we set out to clean, sweep and polish desk after desk after desk, my little brother and I pretending we were the bosses.

My grandmother's name was Marcela, not Marcella.

THE FRUIT TREE THEY MIGHT HAVE PLANTED BEFORE THEY WERE NATURALIZED

16 May 2018

The story goes: the ones who came over here before dishwashers were sold at Simpsons

planted fruit trees that did not die when their own days were done.

You did not ask me about the Serviceberry tree.

I planted that tree for our baby son;
he may have been three by the time the city delivered the lanky sapling.

You needed a wide-angle lens to gauge how many tears would fall when the tree was removed to make way for a garage.

I did not see past the lumps in my neck, the ones that scraped the inside of my legs. I was not a reliable narrator then, and not now either.

I relied on you and the love we put on the mantle. The cardinals flashing, calling me outside

so I could one last time see how tall the Serviceberry had stretched, how regal my son.

DEFEND ME, OR, REGRET

4 July 2018

I.

Don't we just talk around it, I mean, when we meet and then there are the stories and we listen?

(I thought that was a question.)

I have tricked you just like I tricked my own mother and the children I love so much. I want to cry when I remember the days and the nights, waiting for them to come home and probably wondering would it ever end. Didn't you think the same thing, you who are mothers with complicated lives and unclear motives?

And now the waiting has ended but I didn't notice that it really helped.

My underside cringes: still I will be blamed for not knowing this way from that.

Never sure. Wanting my family to return to the same house in the same yard with the same neighbours, the same cardinal. I want the Serviceberry tree to be there on the side of the wooden shed that we lovingly whitewashed. It looked like a shack; it was time to improve, I know, and I get it. But the boards were uneven and shaped by winds.

I cannot really understand who has permission to cut down a tree and who doesn't. There is a subject, but the verb doesn't surface.

In the week that both Kate Spade and Anthony Bourdain—they died. She made my cup and saucer first, green cup, blue saucer. He said, life is already too hard so be kind in the kitchen; I cook for her because I love her, he said, my little girl. He kissed her and served her and spread the creamy blue cheese on a clean white baguette or maybe that was me who did that.

In any case, I am terribly afraid to tell you I am not happy enough to stay here because even though it is true I made my choice, I did not know I could take care of my family or our home. I felt the weight of my neck and my abdomen. I wanted to be at home but did not know how—I had a violent desire to give it all away along with the sorrow and confusion. I burnished the desire to stay so that the disease would have less power over us, you and me, and the children we all love, but without grass, I would walk on something less sentient, and I would not have to see the flowers my mother and my grandmother, on their knees, blind, planted, nor the Serviceberry. Did I really think I would forget that time passes?

[Did I lift the rake, or did I pull it across the back lawn in the sun? Did I see raccoons in the shed, piddling on my essays and report cards mixed in with spiders, all gone now? Is it a crisis, saving the evidence from 1972, or just a colourful habit?]

(I am not sure there should be a question mark.)

II.

I can choose happiness: that is what the heroes who have been protected by history say. Me, I only choose to understand how I can struggle harder against that flap across my eyes. The power of regret of before, of yesterday where we all shared space and time. That part stays still. And yes I chose to abandon my home and they admonish me.

I cry out: I have a reason, defend me. I had bulges that blocked my vision and made me feel alone in front of the fireplace in a dark room even though there was a bright winter sun sparkling on snow. A sleek walnut banister, softened by many stroking hands, built in 1922 they say, oiled and smooth. Stained glass windows at the landing, bright reds and blues, always there to filter out the sparkle and iron it into bars of softer light. Like a child, my mother says, I pout, and wonder why I can't have what I want.

I pouted.

So when I am with you I wonder what we talk around. Is there a sadness and a fear that we share, close to the top of our stories, but still a liner, a filmy present, a plain sadness. I am not talking about intellectual vanity or brilliant neuroses but something light and pouting. Press my hand onto the fabric and tell me you feel what I feel, that no, we are not so different, but neither are we the same. We long for the criss-cross pattern of not remembering too much, and yet never want to forget too little.

When I write I imagine I can tell the truth and yet even the truth stays dry like an empty pie crust. It finds me in the middle of the night when the traffic slows and the neighbours sleep. It tortures me and asks me to weep and I say no no leave me alone. Let me be happy with this room and these walls; let me be.

SAVING SEATS

8 February 2019

We probably always wake up in distress from our dreams. Why else have them, I guess. Are they there to hound us or soothe us is the main question, and I say loud and clear: hound.

I was so grateful to be awake and enjoy those first few moments of realization that I was now in the real world and before, it was a world of my own making of which I knew nothing, a dream world. What a curious state of affairs for the mind that just tries to live well.

I was at a very large event—large in the sense that there were thousands of people amassed in folding chairs and picnic tables that stretched the length of a room as large and high as an airplane hangar. I have been in this hangar before—well, but of course I have because how else would I have known what a hangar looked like. But I misspeak: what a hangar *felt* like.

To be quite frank, I mean something different: I am talking about the dream world. I had placed other figures and interactions in spaces much like this one in other dreams in other times and when other emotions dominated the scene.

In this instance, however, I had left my beloved at the very back of the rows and rows of chairs to mind our bags, afraid we would not have seats if we did not save them—a dreadful habit of humans in crowds to "save" seats for absent guests. Then I began the long walk to the front of the building where there hung a huge screen on which all of us were supposed to be able to watch a special film. In my view, there was no way we would be able to see this screen from our current chairs. I needed to look for our children who may have been able to secure seats closer to the front.

Time passed, and eventually I found my friend, Glynnis, seated in the first row of seats, almost facing me. She smiled and chuckled, as if happy to see me. Beside her were three empty chairs with a coat thrown over them. Beside the coat was my daughter looking glum. I was so happy to see the empty chairs, and yet wondered where our boy was. It was his new black jacket strewn across the chairs; I was sure of that. His sister said: he went to get something.

And these chairs are for us? I asked, with confidence.

She said: no, he is saving them for his friends.

A stone fell in my chest, and I set out on the long walk back to our chairs, and my sweetheart who was saving the seats from which nobody would be able to see the film. I could feel tears welling but I also felt enormous pressure to act as if it was all okay, just like a mom does when she is blue.

Grace was mine and she gently nudged me awake as if to say: don't worry, it didn't really happen that way.

BIG LAUGHING GUY TURNS THIRTY-ONE

4 July 2018

Our son was born on 4 July in 1987. He was a gift. He was very beautiful. As his Tata said, look how gorgeous this baby is.

We brought him from Peterborough to Toronto just as he approached his first birthday.

He knew only one home, sweet and spicy, and he rolled around in his golden pram. Baba bought that pram at Macklem's on Roncesvalles, and she pushed him in it from Windermere to Jane, from Annette to Bloor.

His smile sunk ships.

He loved to be swaddled. Tiny hands peeking over white flannel.

He was Big Laughing Guy; he could smile and laugh in the same breath.

We had to fight over who would get to hold him—his dad, his sister, or his mom.

We never made him sleep in his own bed, but he went on his own when he was bored with us.

He grew tall quickly. He climbed stairs when he was six months old. He stood up when he was seven months old.

He climbed onto the television when we were baking muffins.

When he was nine months old, he walked across the room and giggled through a squeal we had heard before.

When he twirled our hair and kissed our cheeks.

THE NEW BABY AND EMMA GOLDMAN

26 November 2019

The new baby was on the floor in a bassinette and our children's Grandmother leaned over and said to herself, look at the size of my baby boy's chest. It was so broad and big that she knew the baby would not overlook those things that are vital to us and long love. His chest heaved and she felt proud and excited for this new baby, the third of what turned out to be four children. For a while, he was the little one in their family and was, as a result, privy to special opportunities. For example, when he was seven and Grandmother had to stay in hospital for a few weeks, he was allowed to make toast for the family. After his third shift he decided that making toast was not all it was cracked up to be. He phoned his convalescing mother to announce he no longer wanted the job.

I thought it was odd that the baby was on the floor, so I asked Grandmother—which is what we all called her—in which hospital did you deliver this beautiful boy?

She said: it was on Quebec Avenue; it was called the Strathcona Hospital. Our doctor was a comrade, and so we chose him to deliver our baby. This was 1950—only six years before Khrushchev would denounce Stalin in his now infamous speech, "The Personality Cult and its Consequences." As it turned out, the Strathcona

Hospital was located at 32 Gothic Avenue, at the corner of Quebec Avenue, a stately old mansion that has recently been divided into condominiums.

Things change.

Dr. Lowry, if we remember his name correctly, was prevented from securing privileges in the public hospitals. The Cold War was brewing—communist physicians were not highly regarded by the Canadian medical associations, or by others for that matter.

Grandmother and Papa would have a change of heart about the soviet experiment six years later when Hungarians took up arms against the invasion of Budapest and the suppression of democratic rights by the Soviet Union. By 1957, Grandmother and Papa had left the party; Papa's own father, Jacob Penner, was outraged by this decision and for a very long time, could not forgive his son. There was talk about betrayal.

Jacob Penner lived in the North End, Winnipeg—the city to which he had immigrated from Ekaterinoslav, now Dnipropetrovsk, Ukraine,[26] as a young man.[27] Jacob was a devoted city alderman and to the death, a committed communist and active party member.[28] He was an organiser of the Winnipeg General Strike, and founder of the Social Democratic Party and the Communist Party of Canada; he had always chosen the social good over the personal. Although born in Ukraine in 1880, he was ethnically German and spoke *Plautdietsch,* discernibly Mennonite Low German. I have

---

[26] Ekaterinoslav was part of the Russian Empire.

[27] See Cathy Gulkin's "A Glowing Dream: The Story of Jacob and Rose Penner." Season 2, episode 14.

[28] See Stefan Epp's *"Fighting for the Everyday Interests of Winnipeg Workers": Jacob Penner, Martin Forkin and the Communist Party in Winnipeg Politics, 1930–1935,* Manitoba Historical Society. http://www.mhs.mb.ca/docs/mb_history/63/winnipegworkers.shtml

seen Jacob in television interviews and heard his voice; he is always smoking a cigarette and always wearing a dashing three-piece suit and a pressed white shirt. He is a short man, but tall enough to be remembered by a commemorative plaque. It reads: "City alderman, 1934-1962. He dedicated himself to the people of the city he loved so well." Despite his communist calling card, Jacob was highly regarded by Winnipeggers. As the world turns.

Jacob met Rachel (Rose) at a meeting of the Winnipeg Radical Society where, that evening, Emma Goldman addressed the crowds.

Years later, it is said that Grandmother and Papa may have also met at a rally where Emma Goldman spoke. It may have been at a Communist Youth meeting in Montreal, or at the Hygeia Club,[29] or the Toronto Heliconian Club in Yorkville where Goldman warned of the imminent dangers of fascism.[30] If it wasn't Grandmother and Papa, then it might have been Grandmother's parents who did so. That is the way it was in those days. The facts are sometimes exchanged for details that prove the point: the point being, everyone was connected and ended up exactly where their histories had predicted they should be: copulating, reproducing near the source, recreating just lives as close to their loved ones as serendipity and money allowed, arguing for affordable housing, unemployment insurance, free and universal health care while calling for the overthrow of capitalism.[31]

---

[29] See *Jewish Women's Archive*.

[30] Born in Kaunas, Lithuania, Goldman lived in Rochester, N.Y., and New York City, and died in Toronto, Canada, on 14 May 1940. Yet, in accordance with her last wishes, she is buried in Forest Home Cemetery next to the Haymarket Martyrs who were her heroes, just as Emma and Jacob are mine. "Pettiness separates; breadth unites. Let us be broad and big. Let us not overlook vital things because of the bulk of trifles confronting us." And so, the *new baby* was named Gary and he never forgot the wise in the face of the trifling.

[31] See Stefan Epp's article, www.mhs.mb.ca/docs/mb-history/63/winnipegworkers.shtml.

Goldman was nearby; she lived with friends on Vaughan Road in Toronto, a city she complained was "deadly dull." About those speeches that brought together two generations of communist lovers, *The Toronto Daily Star* wrote: she is "a feminine Socrates conducting a brilliant dialogue on high and grave questions of human destiny and human conduct..." Emma Goldman had immigrated to New York City in 1889 in order to escape a violent father and other indignities; she loved America and only settled in Toronto in 1926 because it was "the next best thing" to exile farther from the United States of America. "Her ideas made nations tremble: thoughts about freedom and free speech and free love; about feminism and marriage and birth control; about violence and pacifism and war. She'd been thrown out of the United States for those ideas, forced to flee Soviet Russia, driven out of Latvia, Sweden, Germany ... Canada was one of the very few places where she was still relatively welcome."[32]

It was the anarchist, Emma Goldman, who launched the movement to ban Toronto teachers from using physical violence to "discipline" their students. *The Most Dangerous Woman in the World* died after spending six weeks at Toronto General Hospital where her namesake—Jacob's great granddaughter—Emma, would be born forty-four years later. She had had a deadly stroke, and a few weeks later, the great orator was silenced by a second one. She died at the age of seventy in the house at 295 Vaughan Road, waiting for a meeting to begin. And so here we are now—we follow a straight line from Strathcona Hospital to Vaughan Road, from the heart of Jacob's grandson to the soul of Goldman's legacy, uniting us.

---

[32] See Adam Bunch, "Emma Goldman in Toronto."

REMEMBERING, OR, LOVE

30 September 2018

Her nails were always manicured and painted then, just as now.

My mother's fingers. I can see them and feel them. Often, they are painted purple. The purple nail polish is from her granddaughter's store in Brooklyn. I wonder if my mother likes the colour. Even though I remember that her nails were always manicured and painted when I was a child, I do not know what colour she chose then, when she could see the colour. Perhaps it was the colour of the fifties: Red. *Cutex Salon Polish*, maybe *Laurel* or *Cedarwood*, or more likely, *Old Rose*. Then there was her favourite brand, *Max Factor*: *Hi-Fi Red Contrast*, less saucy, more professional. Yes, that makes sense.

My mother did not play a musical instrument, but her fingers were long and slender. "Fingers like that excuse everything," I read in a novel.[33]

---

[33] See Jonathan Littell, *The Kindly Ones*. The full sentence goes like this: "Fingers like that excuse everything, even being Jewish" (92).

ANOTHER LETTER TO MY MOTHER

2 August 2017

14 September 2017

She was not quite three years old when her mother walked out. Her name isn't important, but you need to know that she had a father who painted us into his future. She always saw more than was clear. She noticed her father's broken heart.

Soon she would have to say: "I have two fathers."

Both fathers are painters, but maybe the painter who stole her mother's heart is more famous than he whose heart was broken. The child we have embraced is now past retirement age. She is my friend, and I know that sounds run of the mill. But most love is run of the mill and therefore satiating in the moment and then again later when twilight falls across our horizon and we wonder: how many years does love take?

She is a true friend: she is kind and generous with me and with others, but by the time I finish writing you will understand this more clearly. How could it be otherwise, you will whisper, because nothing seems obvious when you first encounter a beautiful woman.

My friend's mother was young and beautiful and came from a good family. She was smart and kind then and she is now, too. She knows what happened—but then, who among us doesn't really know? Love is a mutable thing: it has a very high temperature in the summer, but it cools when the water on Georgian Bay tries desperately to freeze. The water generally fails to freeze.

Glynnis Thomas French stands beside her father, Vincent Thomas, who is seated in a low wooden chair at Jacknife Lodge, Nobel, Georgian Bay, August 1953.

The mother, father, and child were at the lodge that blue-water evening. They all went about their business: some painted the scene, some must have observed and maybe looked at each other. The child now says: I know nothing of this event because I do not remember it. The child's father painted at dusk on the rocky shore of Georgian Bay, and so did the other father even as he coveted the trio in dulcet chords.

It was all part of the flow that three-year-olds inhabit with vibrancy when they have no choice. She does not remember her gracious young mother, and into this deficit years of story will later be deposited. Time itself will edit the remaining paucity with loving desire and eternal yearning that continues into the stream, this flow I mentioned before, sweetly moving harmonies.

But I am getting ahead of myself. "Remember" is not the right word really, because she doesn't really remember in the cognitive way— and I always appreciate such profound reminders. Remembering follows a gentle sequence, a journey on which it embarks with irreverence and even heated heart throbbing and toe twitching. The flow carries us along into the next moment and then the next and again another next. Not even a real bomb, not a martini made with ninety proof—no, neither can dam the quiet rivulet or the gray-black torrent that she almost enjoys.

Almost is the not same as "I do," but I am sure you know this. How many girls have lost their mothers when they didn't want to lose their mothers or when they didn't know it had happened? Not knowing is a romantic story. Romantic stories have currency. Yearning is like the breath. It goes in and it goes out.

Had you asked me about my mother when I was thirty-four months old, there would only be an echo of an accolade. I would remember the watery joy between my heart and my soul, the chimera of warmth in my hands, the feeling of inherited or migrant grace.

I am telling you this so you will know that I took this story of my mother with me. It would protect me in later years, those years when the child will find any reason at all to run away from the beloved. My friend was there when my mother's loss stung, but maybe this was just arithmetic. Without numbers there is so much gloss, so much residue, so much shadow.

And yet she remembers she had to cry herself to sleep. And her father sang as he walked in the bush with her perched on his shoulders: "Kisses sweeter than wine" on the rocky shore. He loved his daughter; this does not mean his wife did not love her. By all accounts, this is all you can say.

How could my friend know that she would indeed remember? And what could she do about the memory anyways? Her father's face and his voice are emblazoned on her chest only because that is what I see. We are obliged to ask the obvious question: whose story is this? Is it my beloved friend's or is it mine? Having answered that, you may have to then belabour the basis of friendship that does not stop. Love wounds sweet persons and all others who do not find respect enough to hold balance, to keep kosher, to make confession, to buy time.

Mind you, wounds do not betray love, and now we falter. We are phased. There is a way that novelists are allowed to pretend that what they present to us in final form is not about them specifically. Walk on and follow the storyline best you can, now when there is much less light in autumn.

My friend—let's continue calling her "she"—she loves her mother now, but her chest is laced with white cotton when they are together. When I can make lasagna, I feel her shadow. I share my Kevlar vest with her and she writes letters that no one will ever read. Except for me apparently, or so this story goes.

HIGHWAY 400 TELLS STORIES ABOUT TEENS

10 April 2019

I remember the outlet mall on this side of Barrie, one of the many decorations on the famous 400 Highway, the path to cottage country for those shiny folks who belong in the new world, or look like they belong.

Many city folk travel up this blustery highway to find peace and quiet beside a lake. Does this pattern of escape or vacation mean the same thing to a foreigner? I got a hint of this glorious, complicated narrative one day when the sun was shining and my mom was waiting for her granddaughter to arrive at her cottage, a mecca on Thunder Beach.

Emma always wanted to stop at the mall on the highway, and shop. What fun that was—or so we all had hoped. My wiser side now says shopping with a preteen is never really like the story we like to tell ourselves, or the hope we may have cultivated. Although maybe, in another pitch, it is.

We looked, we listened, we gave her advice, and we purchased the absolute minimum we could tolerate—or to be honest, the absolute minimum that she, the queen of the house, could tolerate. That is such a funny balance, and it might be a universal theme celebrated by others more famous than Shakespeare, such as *Chicken Soup for the Soul*. I am thinking of a theme that appeared in the language of love before teenhood was condemned as atrophy.

Between them and us and it starts: in our own home, under the same roof, with the same blood and a shared complicated history that somehow crossed the ocean and settled in winter. Those cottagers who are the less immigrated might call the interlopers ghosts.

* * *

It was halfway to my parents' place on Thunder Beach—there was no way you could call it a cottage and keep a straight face. This romantic home was meant to be the site, the edge of water where they had hoped they could retire. But things did not turn out that way.

Until that scary moment when we traded that piece of land, we had a place to go as a family, a European family with accents that made no mark on the curves of the bay. My parents got into this stretch of beach by accident, but it didn't matter. Nobody noticed that they weren't really there to belong. But, as you know, on the other hand, that is just silly thinking. Of course, they noticed; but to us, it did not matter until last week when I drove along West Shore Drive and I noticed my father's signpost: this cottage once named *Ellmar* was now named *Lac*. There is nothing left of this family apart from the Mar. How sad it seems. How many more signs of loss can a history absorb without collapsing in a heap of disease, or sorrow, or both? Shopping at the ugly mall with a teenager is certainly a finer way to mark time.

Geographical hot spots make good memories, but they are also unreliable. I have more to write on this topic, but I am tired and can't find the memories to suit the words. So I am thinking, let's go back to the beginning. Is there another way to revive the beauty?

***

Yet one more thing I want to recapture from our shared past as a family. I wonder if it is about being bored and getting a new thing to artificially stimulate interest or the opposite of boredom.

TOO MUCH BEAUTY

28 April 2020

There are many kinds of beauty that are too much.

When you were born, they said, "she looks so wise." The most exciting day it was. You were so tall, so smooth, so attentive. Tata said: "how can one baby be this beautiful?"

Grandmother stayed behind to wait for your birth, to talk to you before anyone else had time to embrace you. Before your dad had any wherewithal, so smitten was he.

When you were five, they said, "she is so poised."

When you were seven, you sparkled in a classroom, excited to find a new problem to solve, causing problems for your friends.

When you were ten, you read aloud in French to younger children, all of whom said, "I want Emma to read to me." Did they like your accent, or your kind manner and impish smile?

When you were a preteen, you cuddled musical instruments, hockey sticks, and ballet shoes. We had considered boarding school, but reneged when we looked at your tidy room, your carefully organized closet, your expanding bookshelves.

"Emma is so nice," the little girls said, and when you were fifteen, you won praise and accepted it with modesty. I remember you calling my name and feeling the pride I feel now as I celebrate your thirty-sixth birthday.

When you were nineteen, we stared at you, your healthy strong body and your luxuriant hair, warm eyes, and long fingers. You used to say, "Granny has nice hands."

You wrote books for us, collected photographs to make our memories stick, and cooked unusual recipes, sweet scents, training us.

Your face is radiant; a bright light in my front-view mirror, and a mellifluous voice, a hearty laugh, and a captivating giggle. In various postures, you are many kinds of beauty, and I am the lucky one.

THE TIME WILL COME: PART ONE

2 June 2020

There is no evidence that human beings approach the end knowing all will be well, that they will move on to the next world where loved ones will welcome them and joy will predominate.

The woman I met at the salon was in her ninety-first year, and very attractive. She had not had children, nor had she lived alone until her husband died four years ago. She did not need to go to the salon in the way that most of us do. Her hair was thick and luxuriant, a kind of greyish blond. When she was younger, her hair reached her shoulders. She didn't believe that, though: she said, when did I ever have long hair?

I continued to meet Maria at the salon, and eventually we would chat after our hairdos were set with gels and sprays. Her hair did not move and now, I am proud to say, mine doesn't either.

Time passed. Eventually I visited Maria at her residence. We would have breakfast together on those days and chat about the weather and the other residents. Maria found the habits of some of her neighbours irritating. I suppose if I had to live in a residence, I would also find fault more easily.

She had met a resident who tickled her fancy. Her name was Adele, and she was thirty years younger than Maria. She was in the residence to recuperate from a knee replacement surgery. So, time came she was able to go back home to a husband and an adult son, who lived in the basement with his fiancé.

Maria was good-natured, really, and wished Adele well but missed her. It was clear that Adele admired Maria, too, and their friendship grew even as they lived apart. Surely this was a lovely opportunity for both of them to enjoy the new spring weather and talk about their next steps. Adele visited often. As different as they were, they seemed to understand something that eludes me: all will be well, they whispered to each other in an otherwise silent encounter.

Maria had been a marvelous cook in her day, and even now she could invent a meal from pickings in her fridge without much effort. She had no respect for cookbooks, mind you, but she watched cooking shows as if they were cartoons.

Adele brought food on occasion. She was Italian and made foods that might have been eaten in Budapest—lots of spices, paprika, more salt than is healthy, cream sauces, cauliflower, and butter. For some reason, she had very kindly prepared butter chicken using sauce from a jar and delivered it to Maria just as evening approached.

Maria tried the butter chicken over rice and called to say: I guess Adele doesn't know how to make butter chicken using the sauce from a jar. It was terrible. There was too much cauliflower, and the texture was lumpy.

I remember what I said.

I said, oh.

I wanted to make something special for Maria, something that might not disappoint. I decided to make chicken that had been marinated in a tangy barbecue sauce: a new recipe from the *New York Times*. A guy named Mark Bittner, I told her, just like Rick Bittner next door. You remember Rick, of course. A good omen. We are sure to like Mr. Bittner's recipe.

She called later that day and said: I had to scrape off all that horrible barbecue sauce. It was full of hickory. But I explained, that is odd, no, we didn't use hickory. We used smoked paprika from the market in Budapest. No, it was hickory, she declared. I said, no, it was paprika. She said, well, it tasted like hickory. I don't like hickory.

I understood, I really did. I just thought I wanted to lie down.

CHRISTMAS MORNING 2012

Linda

Christmas morning we walked through the alley.
There were no cars on the road, and the snow fell fully to the ground.
The sky was grey, and the air filled with the longings of past
Christmas mornings.

I was not alone and would not trade that morning for any other.

Yet families believe their blood makes us adhere.

PRODIGIOUS PEACE IN HUMAN METRE

18 July 2017

We all know what to do when nature's wake-up call filters through an uncovered window or when yawning becomes a chore; we know that at different times in the day we do different things. I have read that this knowing has something to do with the planets and the presence or absence of sunlight in the human metre.

On the south coast of Nova Scotia there are many kinds of unusually large shore birds. These birds have magnificent wingspans even though some consider themselves parasites, brigands, and yellers: hunters and killers. Herring Gulls, too, know what is what and when. We have borrowed the German word for hunter—Jaeger—in order to describe the soldiering gull that pirates food from friendly terns with aplomb, or steals infant birds from their nests. The Long-Tailed Jaeger is a huge bird with a forked tail.

South Shore Gulls march across grasses as if in armies, but for each time of the day, there is a different army, each with its own distinctive uniform, each with a specific call—the morning call is brazen and imitates the timbre of the disagreeable woman I remember as Brown Owl: *hyah*, it screeches. The size of the wandering soldiers appears to vary according to the time of day, too, unless their food source is the key and I can't see that or measure it. Green worms or aquatic invertebrates in the morning; dung and carrion in the evening.

The morning army is white with grey wings and a tail that separates into black and white. Some gulls are mostly white, and they talk like we do when we make claims like: *kak, kak, kak*. But there is an occasional speckled gull in the group, though it still has the yellow bill with a tiny red tattoo at its peak. This bird is mostly light brown with beige and white bits. I am not talking about ordinary seagulls; I am talking about a gull who is so large in the bodice you have the feeling that the next time she bows her head to the dank soil, she will topple over.

As irritable as these gulls sound, they enjoy a soulful community as much as they jostle in it. Once I saw a Herring Gull threaten a minor in the group. Another time I noticed two separate groups foraging near each other and wondered if they had segregated the girls. I think this may be called anthropomorphism. Robert Service is *fey in feather talk* and yet he made my gull speak.

I know that you and all your tribe
Are shielded warm and fenced from fear;
With food and comfort you would bribe
My weary wings to linger here.
An outlaw scarred and leather-lean,
I battle with the winds of woe:
You think me scaly and unclean...
And yet my soul you do not know...

From peak to plain, from palm to pine
I coast creation at my will;
The chartless solitudes are mine,
And no one seeks to do me ill.
Until some cauldron of the sea
Shall gulp for me and I shall cease...
Oh I have lived enormously
And I shall have prodigious peace.

That same cauldron swallows up fishers and trawls on this coast every winter and still women marry these men and wait for their return every seventeen days. Prodigious peace follows. Seventeen days now at home where the wife tempts the man with food and comfort and maybe hopes he has forgotten how to count past ten. The Herring Gull will jostle her and scold the fisher who must live enormously until the next passage.

INJURED SPARROW

19 July 2013

The heat tumbled onto the sidewalk from the greenish lawn.
Our feet were hot and my skin, or was it my brain

     was on fire.

Warm flutters close to the curb scaled the path of our sight.

It was a desperate sparrow
     whose wing was mangled.

She tried so hard to do what she had been told
but the air did not lift her.

Did the concrete burn her feet?

We had to go to work.

THE TIME WILL COME: PART TWO

This whole thing was my fault. I had suggested that last week's rotisserie chicken was my favourite. I wasn't keen on the new barbecue sauce, really.

I HEARD THE LION ROAR

Remembrance Day 2020

We three had had a gorgeous exchange after a rather striking photograph of the 2011 feminist theorists had circulated on email, and only minutes after Sunnybrook had called to say an operating room had become available, and would I like to take it? I thought about the date for a minute: November 25. It was between my birthday and his. I recall this as a pattern: traumatic events occlude our celebrations. The effect is that we must pretend to enjoy each day as it comes, one day at a time as many contemporary self-help gurus iterate. What they really mean is: you are guilty, you are bad, and you must repent.

I am not sure I was asleep, but I was not awake.

Linda, Jeanne, and I were travelling: that is for sure. We had often travelled together when we were figuring out a new project, or editing a manuscript, or, not to put too fine a point on it, trying to find a way to speak to each other about loss.

In fact, we knew little back then about loss. That is my conclusion, even though I am just starting this story.

I was relishing my frizzy observations. I recall that we three, out of necessity, were directed to customs: the lineups of tired travellers that led to what might have been an abattoir during Covid, but we had understood that before we embarked on this new journey (to do work?). Linda and Jeanne were so happy and felt joy at the prospect of yet another voyage, but I did not know what we were going to study.

We three left the airline desk together, and then things began to alter in time and space. I was often separated from Linda and Jeanne because I had to go through customs on my own, but customs was more like a Nazi shower protocol. We were together in a room after travelling on a long escalator, and then suddenly, I was clamped down in a cave-like den—but I was not too nervous because, in the past, we were always reunited after a mishap. I felt tired in the dream and increasingly anxious because I was left behind whenever we were being "checked out" by some vague law enforcement agent yet again.

One time I was with Jeanne and Linda in a small reddish "den," when suddenly a wall came crashing down between me and them. All I could see was red. I was feeling anxious in the dream when this happened, but a part of me said: this is just the surveillance process, so hold on. We will be reunited once the investigations are complete. I was pretty sure of it.

The wall in the red den lifted and at that point, Linda and Jeanne were gone. I was concerned now and so I took out my phone, but it was not my phone. It was Linda's phone, a Blackberry, so I could not phone Jeanne and Linda because I did not know how one dialled the numbers. I was accustomed to an iPhone that I assumed Jeanne had put in her purse for safety. So, none of us could phone the other, I realized: we could not communicate.

At this point, my heart was racing, and I could feel tears forming. I was so sure that Jeanne and Linda would not allow this to happen, but then again, Covid has its own rules, especially at airports. I begged someone to stop this terror, and I woke up. I realized I had dreamed it all and was pissed off. But the upshot is that soon I would have a new tear duct and see so much better without the unchecked flow of tears on my cheek.

BROKEN FICTION: PART ONE

15 February 2020

The only phone number I could remember was Linda's. I was relieved to see the numbers in front of my eyes. I would ask for help.

The person playing the witch gave me her phone so I could dial the number. Terrified, I looked at the face of the Android and saw nothing that made sense. None of the dots connected. All the images blurred across each other and into the rim of the phone. Ultimately, they slid away into the back of the phone. I could not see the back from the front. The situation was irrevocable, I determined when the moment of rumination presented itself.

Not only was my memory slipping—skating across the past—but so was my vision. No eyesight, no foresight, I concluded. Things were fraught.

The scenery was likely violent. I had hoped for distraction, but sadly, none was offered.

In front of my mind was the moseying cat again: fawn-haired and silky, same size as the tiger I had seen a few days earlier. I had to find a way to dial Linda's number; I needed a device. Yet, the truth is, I wanted to run away.

DREAMS

25 March 2017, Brooklyn

A fifth anniversary

I was walking into a very large, airport-like facility with windows all around and people sitting on wooden benches on the edges. Ahead of me were many large machines, airplanes, I thought. I walked toward the machines, carrying a purse on one arm and a large floral cotton satchel in my left hand. As I got closer, I realized the machines were washing machines, thousands of them in perfect rows. I walked normally, as if I was a well person with a purpose. I noticed a woman with dirty blonde hair walking at an angle toward me from the right. She was my height and wore a skirt and flat shoes. I had a concern that the angle of her purposive stride would intersect mine in a manner that would require me to halt. In real life this kind of worldly walking can irritate me if the walker is distracted by a phone call on a cell phone, or if she is behaving self-importantly, perhaps because she is wealthy and healthy. This woman was neither. She began chatting and seemed innocent enough except that she got closer and closer to me. I stood tall and she put her hand on my satchel. I think I pulled away but not sure because she simply got closer and said as if under her breath: give me the satchel. I quickly went over the items in the bag to assess their worth and realized there wasn't much—Helen's clothes, I think—I could have let her have the satchel. But I said no: get away. She put her face in mine and became ugly saying, give me that bag or else. I pulled away again. She said, I will kill you if you resist. Give me the bag.

I was inside a cottage looking out the kitchen window as an army of highly decorated Mongolian horsemen with swords rode past chasing an unknown enemy. I said to myself: you are safe in here because there is water, and a moat between them and us, but I do not know who comprises "us." Soon after an ugly man appeared with a female horse-like animal, missing half a leg, bleeding from its joints, cowering with a dog-like face, as he whipped her. Next, I was at the back of a trolley and Barb was on my left side, another friend on my right. There appeared the old man again, forcing his animal to crouch on the muddy cold ground while he sat in a chair and put one heavy, booted foot on the animal's back. I said something to the guy, like, you filthy pig don't you dare hurt that animal. He came toward me with a shoe's sole in his raised arm as if to hit me. I stood up and crossed my arms in front of me like my favourite emoji and soon after tall Barbara stood up as if to declare war. Then, to my surprise, he backed away.

I woke up.

SPRING BUS STOP

30 May 2017

You may not know this, but there are two bus stops near my house. One of them is at the corner of Ripley and The Kingsway; and one of them is in front of Linda's place around the corner on Yellow Avenue. Either way, it takes very few steps to get on a bus, the 7A. This 7A delivers me to the subway station at the top of Windermere where I used to have a house with a yard and a spring garden. Today it feels like summer, not spring: warm and a little humid, sticky weather. It is a good day to remember that bus stop near Linda's.

I had sat in the blue seats, not because I was disabled, but because the bus was full. Had someone needed my seat, I would have offered it, so don't get on your high horse. I had noticed a very young woman a few seats away with an overly full shopping cart. I had actually tried to help her get on the bus at the subway station while the bus driver yelled at me, at her, disabusing us of our good intentions and making a scene. He said: get off the bus, you. You can't just skip the line and jump on at the back doors whenever you feel like it.

Believe it or not, I thought I was helping by getting on at the back so others who used change or transfers could board at the front with the driver as their witness. Don't *you* like to help others when you have the chance?

But here is the thing.

Only hours before, a streetcar driver had announced, in a warmer tone: all passengers with a Presto card, please use the back doors. True, this was not a streetcar; it was a bus: but my mind did not register a difference until just minutes ago. Difference needs to be studied before it settles in the cool mind. You would have helped the young woman, too: her load was heavy; her tiny frame was strong but not much taller than the cart she aimed to push and lift and shove. She was balancing round fruits that were squeezing out the sides with one hand and the other pulled the cart without making any progress whatsoever.

Let's move on now.

We had all boarded this bus 7A at the subway station, by the way. And after the bus driver yelled at me and also at the young woman yoked to her metal cart—it looked just like the one my papa bought at a garage sale when he was older than I am now—I disembarked and waited in line again so as not to further incriminate myself. It was pouring rain. I just wanted the driver to take my face out of his rear-view mirror. And then it happened: another bus crisis. A well-dressed middle-aged woman flopped in a heap onto the bus driveway. But there was a good outcome: three or four young people ran to her aid in the pouring rain. I stayed in the line-up when I saw the crowd form around her and maybe two or three or maybe four minutes later, the woman stood up and began to walk with slack purpose to her destination. She had floppy legs—no wonder she fell on the rain-soaked sidewalk. This was retributive justice: the bus driver's way was blocked by the incident and he could not, therefore, accelerate his vehicle. Don't worry though: he did not yell at the woman with floppy legs.

Within seconds of this scene melting into its future, the elderly man in front of me said: please, go ahead of me. I said: thank you, but I am happy to be behind you. He said: you were way ahead of me in the line and you should be ahead of me now, too. I smiled and accepted his offer. I didn't want to accept it, but I needed to.

This story seems to be languishing, but it was only seconds ago that the woman with the floppy legs got up off the sidewalk and until then, the bus driver couldn't drive forward into his lane. It is obvious that things were going a bit slowly.

But we eventually crawled up to the main street and then within minutes we were approaching Linda's bus stop—you will remember that I mentioned this stop earlier. No surprise to me, this is where the young woman wanted to get off the bus with her shopping cart. She jostled her way to the front of the bus, past me and past the seventy-five-year-old woman across from me, but she hesitated at the precipice. She asked: can you put the ramp down for me? He said: no, it is broken. My heart was broken because I could feel a storm brewing but I had no evidence.

The young woman had to somehow lift the heavy cart down to the sidewalk. I motioned to help with this task knowing full well I might not make the grade. As I gestured, the seventy-five-year-old woman rolled her eyes, but I thought she was concerned about the bus ramp. I said: it is too bad that the ramp doesn't work for the poor woman. She said: she doesn't need the ramp. She is putting it on. She is a fake. And she smiled at which point I was sure I heard: and I am the real McCoy. I said: I think she needs help. She said: I always take my own cart down and I am seventy-five years old. I said: well, sometimes, age isn't everything. She said: well, it is to me.

OF A PIECE – THE CONDUCTOR

29 January 2019

Two days a week I see this man. He is often alone and walks with purpose. He is tall, and he has an air of confidence. I don't expect him to be a mind reader. But nowadays, one never knows.

I usually hop on a trolley car at the closer intersection. By the time I am seated and have wrapped my thick coat firmly around my hips, a few minutes have passed. I hear parkas and down coats swooshing past each other. They seem to have a life of their own, and they murmur.

Had I not sat down on the stained blue seat, the air would have been quieter, and the sound of quiet thoughts may have floated my way. I knew his lips had moved, but it was not clear he could speak. I witnessed the pressed pleat in his black pants. The pants carved a shape. His long thigh seemed so slender because of that handsome pleat. I took a deep breath. I was sure now that I could hear his thoughts.

Cold wind slid under the windows. The seams that held the glass panels were cracked and dry, just like the skin of a well-used heel, or the whitish edge of a bunion. I was not disturbed by this. I had other things on my mind that day. He, however, was remembering a shaky experience, and his heart was empty for that moment. I wasn't staring, but I saw what happened next.

He had taken a sharp chef's knife out of his jacket pocket, or so he told the officer after the fact. (It must have been in a sheath if he was telling the truth.) The blade of this knife was likely Swiss or perhaps German-made. It was short and shiny, just big enough to slice the inside of his neighbour's palm. Oh, I heard her whisper, but then she screamed loudly, please help me, while the blood appeared to pool in the cup of her hand. The odd thing is I had known it was going to happen even if the others appeared to be lolling about in their own dreams of salvation. Meanwhile she held her palm as if she were feeding wintering chickadees.

The situation was clear to me. I wondered what had intervened between the thought and the act—from the moment I admired the man's pleated pant, and the moment when a silver flash cut through the condensing breath in the car. What had stopped my words when they were most needed? I am aware of what everyone says about hindsight. Hindsight repeats itself though, so let me use it the second time, and the third to make good. Not every violent experience makes a good plot.

There was a lot of blood that day. The skin of the palm is thin, the muscle beneath sinewy, so other passengers were able to see the damage with their own eyes.

But then there was movement. The tall man began walking toward the conductor's chair, so I was afraid for him.

It is unclear which "him," isn't it? The grammar is indirect and leaves a person hanging, not knowing how the conductor fared.

OF A PIECE, STILL THE TALL MAN

30 January 2019

The conductor's seat jiggled when the car hit an ice spot on the rail. His left hand held the steering wheel, but very lightly, shaping the arc it would make next time he had to turn north onto the boulevard. He didn't really greet passengers, but he did release his grip when they boarded the car.

He did not see the tall man approaching. Looking into the rear-view mirror was something he avoided. Looking was rarely just about looking. It usually meant a passenger wanted to talk to him. Wanted to break the noisy silence of a wintertime trolley ride. This kind of motorman would have preferred the wooden cabin of the original Peter Witt tram, private and clean, raked windows at odd angles. In those days, another man collected the fares, a man who enjoyed encounters with commuters, while the man at the wheel sat in peace, in an interior courtyard that swayed.

The tall man's pant leg was clearly not as wrinkle-free as we had imagined. The hem crumpled over his soiled rubber shoes. He did not make a good fashion impression, and still he walked with an air, tossed this way and that by the clanging car, a shimmying car, a car that sways with the rhythm of the town. To forego tailoring on serge pants was a mistake if you walk the corridor of a Toronto streetcar.

He observed the nape of the conductor's neck, hairy and wrinkled, serum-filled blisters lining the collar of his green jacket. The conductor had a skin disease. The passenger felt this observation deeply, like a scourge, a damaging image, and a danger to his kinfolk.

He pulled the conductor out of his seat onto the sandy wooden floor of the car, and there he showed him the knife. Now the conductor remembered what might have gotten him into trouble in the first place: he had taught his children to be good witnesses, not good Samaritans.

WHEN WE ARE THIRTY-TWO

30 October 2015

That was the first time at thirty-two when I wondered about your hair and your smile and the way you leaned.

That evening went on forever, but we kept our distance. You talked about the music, and the meaning of the metres as you wrapped your body around another woman.

I do not remember what I said, but only what I felt, which is how they say it goes when we are traumatized by events that take the floor away.

By the time our cross was brought to bear, we had entered our thirty-third year: our fates were locked.

Here we are now, in the same city, with two, sometimes three or four, angels fluttering in and out when times merge and love re-knots.

A cluster of persons, a knot we are.

FOR HER TWENTY-SIXTH BIRTHDAY

Kim

8 August 2022

Mothers know about the trade

Our kid gets a lover and

then

he

leaves.

It happens

and it turns the wheel as it also takes from the pool of ancient love.

The benefit:

the lover becomes your friend, your muse even,

and

is

loved.

HE HAS A BIRTHDAY THAT WE ALL PLAY

Jayson

21 April 2020

He is in my orbit more than he knows.

He drives a wheel, around the corner, and into our space, as if he didn't know that was what was happening.

He is clearly still assessing us, but at the same time, he smiles when we look across the counter even though we are five hundred and thirty miles away.

Can we say what his qualities are, as if we were simply loving parents?

Not a big mystery but he is too fulsome, too creative, too critical to make a blog, or a persona that I can repeat. His pattern is full of light. He has plied words.

He moves in loving space but is pulled out of his posture by the one we all love equally, and she hovers.

He cries when our mothers die; he kisses us when he finds us; he cooks for us when he knows we want noodles, and even when we are soft and well.

Someone else chose him.

But we love to hold his tall arm, wrap around his torso, admire his dark eyes and wait for the next birthday by his side.

THE VOICE IN THE ANGLE

5 September 2021

There might always be a voice that pops off the concrete in the heat of the sun when you are in the middle of an adventure and illumination is not your first course of action.

I could tell that something was about to happen though. It was a physical sensation that both skin and bone measured. Between me and the concrete sidewalk fell deep rays of pure sun bent by a billowy breeze coming from the west.

I had to hurry. I was impatient to see my beloved and rest my creaky left foot while he poured the watery cocktail into the heavy crystal martini glass. The familiar sound of ice cubes clanging against the sharply tapered glass. Is there a light more beautiful than the way gin with a bloom wiggles across inert cut glass?

And yet sounds abound, don't they? As if by magic, a dulcet soprano voice rocked me gently without my giving it attention. The voice pushed me back from the street curb as if with outstretched arms. Then I heard it:

Well, you are a happy little guy, aren't you?

Of course, I turned, as did you. But you turned the wrong way, toward the little guy in his stroller. By the time the streetlight beckoned me again, the voice had burned its beauty into the sky. Invisible, the voice turned into a refrain I sang in my memory. Where it went after that I am not quite certain, meaning I am uncertain about the source and the evaporation, but not about the person who owned it. I turned for a third time and saw a kind-faced man pushing a stroller; he was wearing sunglasses; he was smiling. He had strong bare arms as if he held hockey sticks when he wasn't strolling.

When the lamp turned green, I started to cross the street with more intention. The bus that stops on Yellow Avenue was approaching and I was not surprised that I had found another good story as a result. This particular story about the voice was already full tilt. I knew in my soul that it wasn't going to find its denouement until I could make the verbs more present. In other words, I was forced to turn my head one more time into the sun and my eyes fell into the tiny angle the light made as it fell on the concrete plane. It was the angle of the "greater than" symbol on your keyboard. The experience only affirmed the prestige of daylight and the wisdom in loitering.

A see-through rainbow bowed into a woman's face. She wore a sunhat. She had saved all of her verbs for dusk when she and her husband would take the child back home.

SKIN PLUS TWO MAKES

28 January 2016

My skin has never been perfect. A friend told me it was blemished all the time but I don't remember that.

A blemish seems to be so important when you are young but not when you are beautiful and lithe and taking care of children.

You have a blemish, too, but you may not see it.

Plus, you have other things. I am not so different a friend told me, but I can't remember why.

Food might be one plus something else that builds hemoglobin and manages lymphocytes. Eating is fun and eating is nutritious. And you know that part.

Vitamins and parts of speech. Or maybe it was minerals, plus one more. Gluten hiding everywhere under the skin and in catsup and vinegar and then more lymph crashing at membranes knocked about screaming and waiting for free health care, waiting waiting and waiting some more, and waiting again plus two.

Another friend told me everyone has swollen lymph nodes because you might have a cold or maybe your body is fighting something. That is not so unusual, mind you, unless you are twenty pounds lighter.

In your skin, where you have that blemish, do you see it, what is wrong with you, in your eyes now.

There used to be many verbs going to work, reading Levinas or Livesay, teaching Levy memoirs, preparing the lecture that always scared me, grading and marking gerunds.

Verbs are less. Adjectives take over when the skin thins and burns or calls out: thin, itchy, hot, itchier, painful, dull, anemic, calling out and out again and again and

Skin plus two does not make sense, makes silence friendlier, makes two points but I often forget where I put them when I have to cry. These poems aren't very good any more.

FOR DORI

30 April 2020

Skin is my medium, the surgeon said

Skin is medium
Like scratchy paper it moves
A new side to face

An abstract painting of a face by Dori Wilson where the right side of the image is obscured by the purple watercolour background.

REMEMBERING, OR, DISDAIN

30 September 2018

So many memories. People say this often, especially when they are older and hoping for something else: that age would not be both the record of remembering and the terrible challenge to recording. We ask someone if they remember this or that, and usually we experience their recollection as true. Unless, of course, we don't.

In the current crisis, Dr. Blasey Ford remembers that Judge Brett Kavanaugh assaulted her with every apparent intention of rape. She remembers that it was Brett with certainty—one hundred percent. Brett Kavanaugh does not say he remembers with certainty—as in one hundred percent certain—but he claims, "it never happened." He has never raped anyone in his life, not Dr. Ford, nor anyone else. Based on remembering, his story is experienced by the Committee of male senators as true. In this context, the memory of the event appears as someone else's entirely, someone who was not with Brett Kavanaugh, and yet it is only Brett whose interest is vested in the record because he will get a full-time job as one of the most prominent white judges in the country, with no need to apply for tenure or tally student evaluations or peer review. His interview is tell-all, and yet, all cannot be told.

It is beyond the scope of helpful wisdom to say this is a sexist context. I have heard it said that if Kavanaugh sexually assaulted Dr. Ford and two or three other women as a younger man, let's remember he is an older man now. Once he had purchased his spouse, his activities were protected by his marriage rights and her potential dignity, never mind the Roman Catholic church.

Deborah Ramirez: Either he did not store the experience of putting his hands over her mouth while he humped her on a bed and Mark laughed with glee, or he is unable to retrieve it.

Jeff Flake [As the elevator doors close]: I understand what you mean, but the point is to ensure that there is more unity in the Senate between the Republicans and the Democrats.

Leland Ingham Keyser: I believe Dr. Ford's testimony, but the problem is I can't retrieve the incident in order to corroborate the intended rape and perhaps murder. I just know she is telling the truth because she has no reason to lie. She is a good person. She is a psychologist. She knows the territory of storage and retrieval better than Lindsey Graham.

Lindsey Graham [Hands rattling and fury in his sloppy cheeks, enters from the centre]: Do you want to destroy this guy's life? Klobuchar works for transparency: give me a break. I have never felt better about the Supreme Court nomination of Judge Brett Kavanaugh than I do right now.

Let's turn to the "anchor baby" for comment.

Rafael Edward Cruz [Seated, but offers to stand, from the right]: Judge Kavanaugh has two young daughters, a ten-year-old and a thirteen-year-old. For the rest of their lives, their daughters will go to school, will interact with people, many of whom are convinced their father is a rapist (*Huffington Post* two days ago).

Those poor girls. We have to hope that they are allowed to store safe interactions with "people," and that they will be unable to retrieve this story in time.

THE RABBIT HOLE

3 October 2017

I thought of so many things I could write about before this moment arrived. There were dreams that offered opportunities and there were feelings that might have had some power were they not so pedestrian. But none of these things claimed me. I knew from the start that the song must write itself, and if it does not have a will to do so, the music is not worth hearing by anyone but me, and even then, there is doubt. Neil Young once said,

> I don't try to think of them. I wait till they come. A metaphor may be that if you're trying to catch a rabbit, you don't wait right by the hole ... And then the rabbit comes out of the hole, he looks around. You start talking to the rabbit, but you're not looking at it. Ultimately the rabbit is friendly and the song is born. The idea is, [s/]he's free to come, free to go. Who would want to intimidate or disrespect the source of the rabbit? And in that way if the song happens, it happens. If it doesn't happen, it doesn't happen. It doesn't matter.[34]

---

[34] See Childers, "Neil Young Explains Songwriting: Never Chase the Rabbit."

Waiting for the rabbit is usually a joy, but this week I have lost my words. My curiosity about the hole under my arm has taken my attention and so I have explored it, looked at the bandages and marvelled that a tube can be attached to a body and not cause pain. This makes me think twice. Is the tube foreign matter? Or is the tube a welcome new appendage by a body that does not want to betray me?

I am taking the high road and sending thanks to my body for accommodations. The body says: life goes on. We do not need the Buddha to repeat this for us. "Life goes on" is simply what our grandmothers wailed over the centuries in faraway lands and in the synagogues and mosques of the future, the churches of grandeur for which we have borne Renaissance art, and, sadly, in the Protestant ethic that has dominated our early dying and our constant search for peace and joy when searching is not the recipe your grandmother memorized.

We return to the simple for solace: a good meal, a fine smile, a duvet. There I see the rabbit and despite better thinking, I do wait by the hole, but I do not suffer.

TO PERFORM

20 May 2020

Don't feel sorry for me, I said.

It is all about being different, the same old argument.

I am different, or just not the same, but your pity makes me want to bite your head off.

Pity is the coating, she said, it is just what we know, or feel when we observe anguish in another person. Another person.

Still, feeling sorry underlines the glee one can take in illness, the specialness of having something nobody else has, the power in so much attention.

The benefit of excuses not to do things, not to give or take, *not to perform*.

I had to ask her to repeat that verb: *to perform*.

To perform illness is my job right now and my duty is to love that job while it lasts.

To perform: what I did all those years when I considered illness an insufficient human weakness and talking about it irritated my sense of propriety and good verdict.

Why won't you commiserate?

Please commiserate. Please tell me you feel that pity you so desire. Please tell me that the cloak that shrouds our anguish can spread your torment across mine in bright layers.

Mind you, I said: I am pretty certain that it doesn't really matter. It has no parity, and human beings are necessarily interested in their own dispositions.

We are in limbo if not apart.

There is only one solution. You can always renege and feel sorry for me instead.

YOU HAVE READ THIS FAR FROM 1320

2015

We had been together for thirty-two years. We are among the famous lovers. We, too, will go to Rome.

"The day that man allows true love to appear, those things which are well made will fall into confusion and will overturn everything we believe to be right and true."
—Dante Alighieri, *La Comedia*, or, *The Divine Comedy*, 1308–1320

TEARS ARE HUNGARIAN?

11 March 2018

Today would have been my father's ninety-first birthday. He *could* have lived ninety-one years: grandmother did and so have many other parents. Instead, he died young and lived his last years in a state of sorrow that I was too preoccupied to honour. As I write I feel the wet of tears on my cheek but I have not initiated crying with my brain. Tears just come. Tears are Hungarian.

My dad's birthday was often a Piscean festival. My mother would make a Dobos torte and a main course my father liked—often cabbage rolls and a roast of some kind or another, smothered in oils and circled by root vegetables spiced with paprika. The torte usually comprised seven layers and was preserved with a burnt caramel topping and a walnut skin. The buttercream held it all together— and everyone would say my mother's buttercream ranked highly. It was only later I learned that the Dobos was not an old recipe, but rather an 1885 solution to confection that otherwise needed refrigeration.

When I miss my father, it is not because I long for his company. That would be a lie, because mostly I worried about him and then made fun of him so he would laugh. Visits in the final years of his life had a stinging quality: he could only stay with us for fifteen, twenty minutes at a time, and then he would generally say: I am hurting. I must lie down. And he would disappear.

But one thing never disappeared, never changed: there was always music. There was music in the living room. Hundreds of CDs carefully organized in a cabinet meant for LPs—and yet there were plenty of LPs, too. In the kitchen my mother would be listening to *Breakfast Classics* on Radio 96.3, the playlists for which I have in time come to love. My mother waited with bated breath for the unsuspecting Bill Anderson to play Dvorjak: then she would revel in correcting him: DVOR-YAK, not DVOR-JAK.

My father's room, on the other hand, was anything but laconic and pure. All I remember now is *Tears of a Gypsy*. Side One began with my father's theme song: "*Keresek egy csendes szugot*," or "I am looking for a quiet corner, a hidden corner."[35] My handsome, charming father could not travel far to find that hidden place even though Toronto always felt foreign to him. He resorted to a blue living room and imagined that seated across from him on the blue sofa was Lendvay Kalman, a fiddler he fancied in his heart and soul was brethren.

---

[35] I'm looking for a quiet corner,
hidden corner, where no one can see,
There I want to forget many, many painful,
many sad things.
I would like to say there
along with softly crying music:
Once upon a time there was an unhappy,
unhappy poor man
who was not needed by anyone on earth.

I'm looking for a blooming rose
in the gloomy autumn sun,
I'm looking for a name on a tree that
I once secretly carved into it.
I would like to say there
with the rustling of a yellowed leaf:
Once upon a time there was an unhappy,
unhappy poor man,
who was not needed by anyone on earth.

My mother in the kitchen bathed in light classical sounds; my father in the living room bleating melancholy Roma chords.[36] The two kinds of sounds blended, but also scorched each other's edges, sometimes creating entirely new sounds. A joint venture: my parents' afterglow. Something to cover up for the heartache, the quiet violence, the noise and without a doubt, the extreme passion and knotty, prickly love. It is about time I listened to Kalman again: those whining fiddles. One thing about Roma stories: they harbour no curiosity about a life hidden. It is all out there in front of me where I can see it, and where it is so obviously worthy of honest respect.[37]

---

[36] Romani and Hungarian languages are often mixed and used interchangeably in the present era in the former Austro-Hungarian Empire. Emperor Joseph II prohibited the use of the Romani language in 1783. The penalty was physical torture: 24 cane strokes, explains Tess Lulu Orban.

[37] https://www.romarchive.eu/en/music/europe/romani-music-hungary/

ONE: TURNING AND PULLING

9 January 2019

It never seems right. Or it doesn't seem enough. Here we are enjoying the day and another person, a loved one perhaps, is preparing to die, and around the corner, another hides her tears. I wonder: what should I do when I see the anguish?

There are times when I assume it is like a broken dinky toy and I take it to my dad and he will get a set of small pliers and then twist this way and maybe again until voilà it is fixed. Here, I say, take my pliers my friend, and worry your hand around the red plastic-coated handles until it happens, there is a match, and you feel the fire of relief. Grief is a woe we always *say* we can share. Alone, grief is sultry; but together, it is idiom, and it declares itself: here I am and don't you dare ignore me. True, grief and woe natter and gossip, hold hands and make promises they rarely keep.

Just one turn for *spray*; two turns for *stream*, they write on the square green lids that dress the nozzles of plastic bottles of cleaning fluid. But we are not really talking about a nozzle, as such, but a trigger that the housewife pulls, and she bends over to reach the countertop or the floor, and nobody can see that there are tears dropping. She is likely alone, remembering what it was like when her children were little ones and life was in the front.

She knows that nightfall is imminent and so she chooses to spray again as if she doesn't understand why there is a stream option on the green lid. The children's sweet voices wake her, and she wonders, where are they now? Do they remember me like I remember them, she asks, but the reply is in a code I don't quite understand.

Could you please turn it to the *off* position now so I can rest these eyes?

TWO: AND THEN THERE IS LOVE

It is not really enough to clean the countertop when I see another person's anguish, even though it would be marvelous if the shiny new surface covered up the old one, no scuffs or chips, no memories of the bad sort. The trigger would be pulled and it would work, yes, it would resolve the agony of dying too soon or too alone or losing the breath. In my mind, maybe we could read more Ursula K. Le Guin, or perhaps her followers, knowers of the lost ark who in youth feel no anguish.

Yet, it is still not right to enjoy skating on the pond on a sunny day when I know that an aging mother's breath is fading, and a dear friend's T-cells have backfired yet again in that way that signals the failure of medicine, the failure of science to trump passion and fear, kindness and feeling, pity and caress.

There must be a way to show our love without making it a smarmy deal. There must be a way to take away the pain in, say, the left ankle and the right hip so that the boy-child will only have two surgeries instead of four. Wearing splints on his legs at night, I pretended not to see him. How cold I must have seemed; how horribly alarming for the boy; how carefully I loved him as I attached the splints on this ankle and knee, and then that one, forcing the leg to remain rigid as it tried so desperately to sleep, and my mother waited and wept. I was inadequate, but I did love.

I needed someone to tell me about pain when I was little and sweet and meant no harm. I needed someone to tell me I did not need to be so careful, shrewdly delicate, deft; that we would all survive for a time, for a short time maybe, but we would still have candlelit meals together and wait for my mother to deliver the buttery perogies and sour cream. My father, he would deliver the Hungarian pear brandy and my Slovak grandfather the Tokaji wine, as if honey soaked, rated by the number of baskets of grapes it took to produce the special sweetness.[38] "How many baskets did you use?" the owner asked the picker. These are the gifts of immigration, I thought: sweetness, light, wine, then noodles.

My Zedo preferred the sweeter, purer noble version of the scarce Furmint grape, so eventually he asked me to buy the higher grade of sweetness—and therefore, a higher quality of wine. For me, this signalled a great thing and a sorrow: how many grapes poor farmers bent their backs to pick, and I always felt the bend, the worry they must have suspected in the glorious fields just east of the poppy-lined Slovak border. How many times have they been paid to field our hesitations, our uncertainties about the harvest, the language they spoke, the hearsay about climate? The Tokaj-Hegyalja region where the specialty grapes are grown is a borderland—my father's feet are planted on the Hungarian side; my mother's, the Slovak side—one hundred kilometres to her home from the vineyards; one hundred and eighty-eight to my father's. This wine is full of the appetite and the indignation so familiar to drinkers who inhabit the foothills of the Carpathian Mountains.

And then the anguish appeared, and I learned, huh, it might only be about me. Not about the others at all. Just a metaphor for the anguish of those who love.

---

[38] Sweetness is measured in *puttonyos*. Six puttonyos is equivalent to one hundred and fifty grams of residual sugar per litre, for example.

COTTAGE STORY, AUTUMN

November 2018

Yesterday the path to the edge of the bay was barely visible. The sky was overcast, and there was a breeze that made the treetops shiver, bending this way and that to meet up with a sunbeam.

Today the path is clearly outlined, and I had no part in painting this picture. I was not around then; I was sleeping in a large bed. I had gone to be with him, but I never saw him in that huge bed, never mind touched him. He was really very far away. I thought if I could make it to morning, things would be the same again and the morning sun would once again shine on the pathway I so longed to follow.

"Today," I wrote, "the sky is overcast." Even as I read this line I have to wonder: why if the sky is still overcast, can I see the path so clearly? On either side of it there are tall coniferous and deciduous trees that are so obviously used to living here alone and having the sky to themselves.

I don't usually find such geographical details interesting. I don't appreciate writers who spend time describing "rosy-fingered dawns" or "this most excellent canopy, the air." I am more interested in normal words that act out of character.

What's so funny about that?

For example: why when the sun goes to bed does sorrow seem deeper or darker? Loss creeps into my sleep and shakes me up. I want to forget about my mother and my father and my brother then, but these beloved persons hug me and kiss me, they take care of me, they fix my broken hand mixer and brush my hair. They are my culture. They eat with me, foods that my neighbours find too fatty or too creamy. Too many hot paprika peppers.

I want the ghosts to disappear so that I can feel ordinary feelings tomorrow, but they are stubborn lovers and enjoy making their mark. When my brother died, only my mother was there, already blind and so fearful, so sensitive to the past in a way I ignored. When I spoke about him in spite of the priest declaring Roman Catholics don't give eulogies, I said: when I was little, I used to wish that I could have been the one to get his disease, or at least that I could share it. That way I would know how he suffered from the inside. "I have pain," he whispered. Small-boned, tiny, young features, a soft voice.

It hurt so much when I looked at his misshapen wrists and ankles. My young girl's eyes only felt the pain more, just like when I figured out cows were slaughtered by humans without anesthetic so that we could eat them. From cows, we got a different thing, or so I thought. It was called meat, not cow. Another mammal hit it over the head with a hammer and then took a sharp knife to its throat. The animal shivered when s/he saw the killer and soon after entering the squeeze chute, the sentient creature released endless amounts of cortisol.

Sadly, I forget how this story ends. But I do know that when characters in a story walk toward the bay—I mean toward the water—the story is less weighty if you leave your shoes at the side of the path where the sand swells outward. The sand billows, I guess.

THE CALL ABOUT MY DEATH

15 September 2019

Gary was playing the guitar in the locker when I got a phone call from the Ajax Cemetery—where my mom, my dad, and my brother are buried.

The caller said his name was George Hazimeister (I think), and he said he was going through his files on my mother's contract and saw that I was the main contact person. At this point he was awkward in his discourse and said that he did some looking around—he could find my father's gravesite and my mom's. Then I added: and my brother's is there, too, beside the Mahaffy concrete bench. He said, yes, but there is no gravesite reserved for the main family member, Maria Papp, so I thought I should phone the number on file to see what happened here. He said, what is Maria's circumstance? and I added, you mean, am I alive? I was laughing at this point.

He did not chuckle much, but then said, we need to discuss plans with you because your mother left a space for you in her purchase, and other customers would love to use it. Will you be coming to rest with your family?

I said, I have my own family, too, and although I love your cemetery, I do not want my children to have so far to travel to "see" me if they ever want to chat after I die. I want to talk to my mom and dad and my brother often, but I don't drive, and I can't get out to Ajax easily—so I see my first family less than I would like. I have children in Toronto, and children in New York City, so Ajax Memorial Gardens is not convenient.

He said he understood, but spots in Ajax were at least thirty percent cheaper than spots in Toronto, so I should consider this fact before I make a final decision.

I said I appreciated his counsel, but I had another plan, and I also had a husband and four children to consult. I want to be close to them, which does not mean I want to be separated from my parents and brother. I said, I want to discuss this with my husband and kids (hoping he would say goodbye).

It sounds like you are not certain about what to do, he said, so let me reiterate, buying land for burial in Toronto is very pricey.

I said, I have some environmental concerns about buying land to bury me.

He said, so you want to be cremated.

I said, not really sure about that option either as it has some disastrous effects on the environment, too.

He said, I think you might want me to call back in six months so we can counsel you further because you sound very unsure.

I said, I am very sure, but my wishes are close to my heart, and I don't want to discuss them with you.

He asked if he could call again, and I said yes, because believe it
or not, talking to him refastened me to my mother, my father, and
my brother.

PURPLE MOTH

19 September 2020

Words are never quite good enough.

There are so many planes on which thinking takes place. Then there are all those intersections with feelings that have been left just lying there, as if immobile.

I saw inside the dream at the time but then time passed.

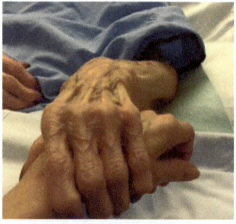

A pair of hands holding onto another. One hand is thin and wrinkled and belongs to a person lying in bed, wearing a blue hospital gown. The other is younger, being held.

The only memory I can imagine is the one about the wings of a purple moth. When the moth approached the bedsheets, its wings became paper thin. Translucent, I could see your face on the other side. I jostled awake, grabbing your hand. I knew that if I squeezed too hard you would cry in pain.

To me, this image was fully mobile. It means you are gone, there is no hand to hold, and time has replaced your beautiful face.

I would wake up in a purple haze, the heart-shaped wings of a moth near my cheek.

I learned you had sent this tiny creature to intrude on my life instead of using words to speak to me. You said: but darling, you know my words are gone now. They were never the whole story anyway.

SO, WHAT IS THE PURPOSE OF OUR LIVES, SHE ASKED

19 November 2016

A purpose is not what I want to think about, too purposive, and meaning sounds a little too precious. But I know what she means.

I have wanted to write about an idea since the last infusion of chemotherapy. But I was too busy in our home with everyday chores and joyful works. I ironed the sheets and pressed them into the mattress for our next guests. I drank martinis made with Hendrick's, just the way I like them, instead of using a cheaper gin. I planned healthy meals and cooked them for us, serving them on the black glass tray.

What though is more joyful than writing? I think it is more joyful to stay away from writing whenever I can make a list of chores that is longer than the hours in the day. Something stops me in my tracks. Ideas are too urgent; thinking is too pleasurable; writing is nearly too important.

When I go into that part of my head that says, "Write, now!" I have a few minutes to think about who is speaking and what are her attributes. I often begin to admire the beauty of character, that feature that distinguishes one of us from another: those contours that differentiate me from you. Character that is especially pokerfaced.

Character that does not reveal itself in and through daily encounters and yet remains stable and intact despite vicissitudes that force our legs to walk this way, then that, and is always revelatory.

As much as I try to cultivate a pokerfaced character, I am not a disinterested party. My interest is virulent, yet mutable and unruly. No big secret gets revealed, though. Instead, the armour that the ego enjoys and despises simultaneously protects the (fabric of) character in its worst moments and betrays when needed. It is the betrayals that interest me. And so I ask myself the questions:

—if I write this "important" thing, can I keep to my stealthy predilection of "do not read this once it leaves you"?

—can I still say with all sincerity that all writing is a plant? It is planted in the soul before writing exists; it cannot be excised when the writing begins because it is already embedded in the hand that holds the pen.

—in other words, can I claim that no, this is not more autobiographical than Elizabeth David's very first publication, *A Book of Mediterranean Food*, 1950, the year I was born? The one that was written in the metre of recipe with few standard cookery measurements, preferring as she did the less scientific "a handful," or a "half a tumbler." Let's not forget it was published *after* she and her lover, a married man, parted in Cairo where they had been living together after a romantic, long sea voyage. They had wintered in the Antibes on their sailboat, the *Evelyn Hope*. The boat was impounded in Italy; later the couple was forced to flee Greece when Hitler invaded. But then here is Elizabeth David in her kitchen, a country-style kitchen but she wears spike heels and sips wine. She has a hairdo.

Elizabeth David, dressed in a pristine white apron and kitten heels, holds a glass of wine standing in her country-style kitchen. The kitchen is filled with breads, fruits, oils and other ingredients. (Courtesy of the Estate of Elizabeth David)

(David died in 1992, shortly after sharing a good bottle of Chablis and a plate of caviar with friends.)

I hold too tightly—like you—to "beliefs" that have to be sifted in the sifter; beliefs that are rooted in opinion need to be swaddled and then stored until they grow up and no longer fit into the shabby clothes of opinion and instead become fibrous, threads in the fabric.

IT DIDN'T START WITH ME?[39]

2005–2022

The First Stanza

"Notes/Memos"

I can remember a page, the words at the top of the page are what I really mean. It was a page in a lined diary, and in it I must have written this piece by hand, and then years later, removed the page. I found it among many other pieces of evidence in the boxes of writing I had saved over the years. I had not saved most of the diaries; I remember shredding the ones I found in my desk. I burned the ones I thought were dangerous when I moved back to Canada from Budapest in 1979. So—I had this thing—writing a diary and then saving it and then destroying it. This one longer lined but unfinished diary entry I saved, probably written in 2005, because that is the year my father died—yes, it was June 12 in 2005. I want

---

[39] The title of this story is a nod to Mark Wolynn's *It Didn't Start with You: How Inherited Family Trauma Shapes Who We Are and How to End the Cycle*. Thanks to Emma Hapke and Gail Lindsay for illuminating discussions about Wolynn's thesis. Thanks also to Marsha Lederman who invokes the power of intergenerational trauma when she has the brilliant audacity to ask: "had Hitler ruined my marriage?" (7).

to read against this piece, but first, I need to transcribe it. I will keep to the original for as long as possible, but make no promises:[40]

> Usually, we write biographies to tell the story of a life. A life to which we have no special rights because it is not our own. The biographer is not expected to know her subject in real life, though sometimes she most certainly does, for better or for worse. But there may be a starting point here that we do not acknowledge, one that is more charming. Is it possible that the biographer is a pretender, writing about another person when she would really prefer to write about herself, but can't bear the attention that act would create. She longs to tell her story, mind you, but is also unable to provide the coherence a reader demands of a wayward subject, one that is mid-life, not end-life, and most certainly not dead—as many biographical subjects are lucky to be. [By this line it is clear my father is the *intended* subject, not his daughter.]

> Winging her way toward some kind of psychical catastrophe, she begs off and instead waylays her angst in the story of her father, the most complicated of heroes. What could the father have been, done, seen, had he lived longer?

> What could the daughter have been, done, seen, had she lived better, still rooted in the patriarch's life? A woman who raises children without her father feels his loss at particular times. There really isn't a pattern to those times: indeed, they steal your attention when you least expect a thief. The times speak the same message: *without the patriarch, you have no roots.*

---

[40] When I do remember and can stop myself from being immersed, I have encased my current additions or editions in square brackets, although these shapes may have slipped into parentheses on occasion.

Your progeny floats; you do not know your roots: where do you come from? Who are your brothers and sisters? Where do they hail? How do they live without you?

It is hard to write about my father without getting misty, but I can't say more about this just yet. Without him here as a figurehead, the question of origins burns.

This is not a [simple] story of the psychological and historical consequences of immigration, but rather the story of a family ragged at the edges, without a centre or a root.

It is as if I want to say that while my father lived, I, too, lived, because I was legitimately rooted in a family, a paternal culture whose fibres were weak, tenuous, feminine, and tormented by breaks in lineage, chasms between fathers, loss of the mother/s forever [still there was a shape to the larger unit. The shape was orderly.]

The torments were handed down to me, I think. When my father died, my poor mother began to flail, also looking for roots but finding none.[41] In fact, she may not have looked so much as she refused to see, not interested in the historical narrative that would provide the coherence of time and place she needed to face her present [or so I imagine].[42] Strong fathers just state what their roots are, or make them up:

---

[41] Her mother and her mother-in-law both never saw their mothers again after leaving their homelands.

[42] My mother was born in Stare, now in the Slovak Republic. She left when she was a little girl, but her girl lived in that village often for weeks at a time. In other words, I know the place better than she can remember it.

I come from X, a land of wise women and men, where my father was a well-loved XX, my mother a kind XXX, a well-placed entrepreneur who watered her plants and fed her darling children, three of whom survived, and they all lived happily ever after in the old country.

[Here there was necessarily an intermission]

[The intermission produced an interruption:

Strong fathers also build their own homes to set down their roots and provide a centre to a context.

To wit:

A man and woman sit on the front stoop of their unfinished home, accompanied by their small, black dog. A vintage car sits in the driveway to the right of the house.

I found this photograph in one of my father's many photo albums, all of which were bequeathed to me when my mother died a few years ago. I asked my aunt about the house, and she said that my grandfather (on the right of the stoop, my grandmother on the left, and the little black spaniel I remember as Blackie beside her) and my father built this house three or four houses from the Garden Centre on Bering Avenue, just west of Islington and south of Bloor Street. With the photo in hand, I went looking, and although it was further from Islington than my aunt remembered, I found the house at 214 Bering Avenue. You can see why it was easy for me to find.

Easy for me to identify.

The front door and garden of a war-time, bungalow style home. The plants in the garden have grown so tall, they obscure the bay windows. A small, black toy dog sits in the front window.

I visited the house a few times and noticed that the curtains were always drawn, but this time they were not *fully* drawn. In between the two panels of drapery sits a tiny black toy dog with a head that bobs. The new owners must have liked Blackie a lot, so they moved him from the cold stoop into the cozy living room of the house my father made.

The Second Stanza

My father's birth and childhood remain a near-mystery to me. Although I asked, answers were not always forthcoming. I had better luck asking my father's first cousin about his family, about her family. My father's early life is in between mountains and plains. My father's early life is between languages. He spoke Hungarian to his mother.

Like many others from the region, my father's birth certificate says he was born in "Huszt, Czechoslovakia"—the city's name is written in Hungarian, as you can see, but a current map says "Khust, Ukraine." Maybe it was Ruthenia.

So many spellings to choose from. So many languages to hear.

His cousin's family—let's call the cousin Elizabeth—like our own, was troubled, ripped apart at the seam by some great sorrow. Or an angst that had history, or hearsay—how can the New Country children ever know? Elizabeth's story begins with her own mother's death during her birth in 1918, and her father's philandering during her childhood. His behaviour resulted in his alienation and separation from his daughter. Elizabeth is my grandmother's niece. My grandmother's name shifts: Margaret/Maria/Marketa. So many names to choose from.

Marketa I will call her, but her birth name is Maria; she had immigrated to Canada in 1928. She disembarked the *Aurania* in October of that year in the port of Quebec City with my father, Josef.[43] Marketa's first baby, also named Josef, died soon after his birth. I think "soon" means "a few months later," but really, who knows how to measure the dénouement in this tale?

Marketa and Joseph Kadar arrived in Quebec City on 14 October 1928 aboard the Aurania

A large, transatlantic passenger ship sits in the still waters of a harbour. Its decks are filled with people and billowing steam.

Eventually, my grandmother would sponsor Elizabeth's immigration to Canada. Elizabeth arrived in Montreal, having disembarked in Halifax, or maybe Quebec City. There were stories about suitors who were Hungarian, but Elizabeth chose a Polish gentleman and they moved to Winnipeg, far away from family. This was surely

---

[43] I was able to read the Manifest for the Aurania and both my father's name and my grandmother's name (this time, Marketa) were listed. I do have the evidence somewhere.

a loss for my grandmother and probably for Elizabeth, the two women who shared a complex identity, neither of whom had mothers to speak of.

Margaret's [Marketa's?] mother never spoke to her daughter again—so the story goes—because she chose a charlatan for a husband and left the mountains for the greener pastures reported to have lined the new world. I have the dowry record to prove it: he gave my great grandmother a horse, a cart, a series of agricultural tools, the nouns for which I cannot transcribe or translate.

See what I mean.

***

Why don't you translate?

CULTIVATING GULLIBILITY [44]

Part One: Dross

I am looking for a less flappable way to inhabit an unwell body in a well world. I have an old red flashlight that I have used in the past when wounds would not heal and I could not see the forest for the trees.

Currently, the future is not clear to me. I almost don't know how to talk about it.

My words have escaped into some ether that hovers in and around renegade cells and I cannot seem to bring them back intact.

Their contours have altered; their attachment to good thinking and generosity has receded; their dressings have been stored away in a hope chest with other adverbs.

There rests my own mother's soul, tortured, laid out like a bride's linens. It has embezzled its own consciousness and escaped into a nether world where memory is edited; where killing machines are oiled in the basement and potions are disguised by rogues in white coats who say they are healers. Sometimes the job is done from on

---

[44] This piece appeared in *Life Writing Outside the Lines: Gender and Genre in the Americas*, edited by Eva C. Karpinski and Ricia Chansky, Routledge, 2020.

high and patients with impaired vision are pressed into columns by jealous muses. Shoved onto the roof. Pushed to their deaths below. This story is shocking but it was told with conviction.

Who, then, will care for this poor woman who, in her more cogent moments, can express with verve and excessive imagination the degree to which she distrusts her firstborn?

Sad and feeling alone, she talks forward and remembers backward, but cannot make the two directions meet in what is here. If today does not fulfill, why wait, she thinks.

It would be easier to narrow the focus of the beam on some made-up idea about profundity. I have heard things like: (incurable) cancer made me strong; or, leukemia is my teacher; or, migraine illumines superficial psychic flaw. I will belong to the world of the well again very soon if not next year, or maybe the year after.

All of these subjects in one story are almost too much for me. If we can meet before night falls, we can share a sofa on the main floor where the remainder of us are hidden in plain sight, where the unwell pretend they are normal, included, hopeful and well. Maybe then I won't have to think about this stuff anymore.

Part Two: The Shimmy of Limits

When we have lots of money it is easier to sustain illusions about others and ourselves. When we have lots of good health, we are more likely to do the same.

Sometimes we come to rely on crutches that appear to sully the medical model of clean, socialized Canadian medicine, medicine that includes legal opiates for the ones who act normal, hide their anguish. Those of us fortunate enough to develop addictions in lieu of excessive wealth or death-dealing disease imagine the calming illusion of control over one's life. I would have preferred an addiction, or even wealth, but I got the disease part.

So I can join the crowd and whine about the flaws and the faults of the addict: the cost to society of incarceration, hospitalizations, employment insurance. Worse still, those who believe they do not have addictions have the same psychic yearning: to feed the illusion that we are healthier or better adjusted than the ones we call addicted, or even so well adjusted, we don't get cancer. Heck no, I don't use crutches. I make money; I am healthy. I have accrued expertise. It is okay that I can't say that anymore.

In our most righteous countenance, we rail against the dreadful self-harm the addict performs. This fact of social life can create a kind of social nausea or a headache much like the one Joan Didion describes when she gets a migraine.[45]

We need to purge the addict from the neighbourhood. We need to clean up the parks. We need to arrest the lonely bums who sleep on sidewalks. Otherwise, how will I walk on the thoroughfare here, or what about over there where the snow is falling in front of the theatre? Or on my way home tonight?

In the silence, the quiet in which we can do little else but think, both striving, and martyrdom evaporate. At dawn it has not been decided what is true and what is false.

So this is what Frank Seeburger said: "thinking is a sabbatical practice, the fruit of rest and not of restlessness. It begins only after we are set free to go home to a place ... of serenity rather than drivenness." The only good thing about being really ill is that you cannot easily continue

---

[45] Didion, "In Bed."

to be driven. (But that doesn't mean that you think more: it mostly means you feel too much.) "Really," the philosopher continued, "to ask a question is to give up the illusion of already knowing the answer, and to give up the sense of control that comes from such an illusion. It is to become, instead, open to learning, ready to be taught—already underway."[46]

Part Three: The Woman Who Sounded Like Zsa Zsa Gabor[47]

Okay, well, I think about this idea often, this idea that I have harboured the illusion of already knowing the answer when, of course, I could not have known it. But it was a woman whose voice was like my grandmother's that switched me over. Ever since I read the story about the inert—or maybe just silent—woman who had been transported on May 16, 1944 from Pécs—or maybe it was Pest—and who, likely one of the few tattooed,[48] worked the Kanada Kommando detail at Auschwitz-Birkenau. She told the story of the October 7 uprising gone wrong. She talked like Zsa Zsa Gabor.[49] She had witnessed the entire tragedy and had survived to tell the tale. The interviewer listened with attention, as would you.

---

[46] Seeburger, "Thinking Time, Drinking Time: A Beginner's Thought."

[47] There are many women who sound like Zsa Zsa Gabor, some of whose names we will not know, and some of whom found respite in Canada at some point after the war.

[48] Getting a tattoo can be seen as a good sign in the camps. If I were to be killed upon arrival at Auschwitz-Birkenau, I would not be processed first for tattooing. Thus, the tattooed person lived beyond arrival.

[49] Although I do not have a physical body in mind when I refer to the Zsa Zsa person, I do have two such persons in mind: Ibolya Szalai Grossman (author both of *An Ordinary Woman in Extraordinary Times,* and, along with her son, of *Stronger Together*); the second person is Elisabeth M. Raab, author of *And Peace Never Came.*

The interviewer was not alone. Fellow historians at Yale had assembled a scholarly panel to sniff out real history, something one might actually prove. They needed a true catalog of the events. We will add this person's story to our collection, they may have dreamed, and then we can document it, they might have judged. We can also then enlarge the picture, persuade the employer. But the interviewer, this historian about whom I speak in passing, had been deported from his home a young boy in Czernowitz, Romania in 1942: not that it mattered, or maybe it did?

I wonder: maybe Zsa Zsa was sixty-seven years old or so when this whole thing ignited. She proclaimed: what a scene when the *four* chimneys blew up, rubble everywhere, prisoners running, guards shooting, friends burning. But me, she said, I couldn't run; I was busy sorting clothes and jewels after my compatriots had been removed. I was not a martyr; I did not help collect the gunpowder like other women. You should remember that one of the Wajcblum sisters was not hanged on January 5, 1945: Hana Wajcblum. She died in Ottawa in 2011 as Anna Heilman.[50] (In between she had other names, such as Hanka or Chana Weissman, or Weissblum.)[51] She had a good job, too, in what she called the "shit Kommando."[52] Sorting was a good job. Other peoples' children had relinquished their satin yarmulkes and their shawls and clips: the adults, they wore silks. The silks were torn but had hems. I found rubies and laces in a red taffeta hem, she said.

---

[50] Her obituary reads: "Heilman, Anna, Jewish Resistance Fighter (December 1, 1928 – May 1, 2011). Anna Heilman (nee Wajcblum) died peacefully in Ottawa, Canada on May 1, 2011, after a short illness. Born in Warsaw, Poland, Anna participated in the 1943 Warsaw Ghetto Uprising and as an inmate in Auschwitz helped smuggle gunpowder with her older sister, Ester, for the October 1944 Sonderkommando uprising. Anna was predeceased by her mother, Rebecca, and father, Jacob, both murdered in the Majdanek concentration camp (1943); by Ester (executed as a Jewish resistance fighter in Auschwitz [1945]); by her oldest sister Sabine (1995); and, by Anna's husband of fifty-eight years Joshua Heilman (2005)."

[51] See "Witness statement from Marta Bindiger Cige."

[52] Ibid.

I stole things from the suitcases for my comrades. I saved lives, yes, I did. Yes, four chimneys blew up; it was such a thing that day. Irina was punished for stealing, in the courtyard of Block 11 where the hanging post had been planted in cement warm enough to spread in December in Poland. Anna watched. There were two performances: one for the day shift; one for the night.[53]

Maybe *S. S. Aufseherin* Alice Orlowski did it but she died in 1976 anyways. Alice worked hard. She hated the Jews, she despised the Gypsies, as required. They say she softened in January 1945. But they said that about Hermine Braunsteiner, too, the one I knew best.[54] For her bestial crimes, Braunsteiner was nicknamed "The Stomping Mare."

The woman who testified against Alice had worked in the Kanada Kommando. She edited as she relived the day. But she could not edit the memory of how it felt. She refused in her mild way the warrant for her death. It did not matter that we were not there then to hear her.

Dori Laub did not trespass that chasm between what the sorter-woman knew and what she did not know, could not know.[55] He said: how could it be otherwise? How do I know what I do not know? Only she was there to witness the explosion. It must have sounded like four chimneys. It would be better if it were four and not one, wouldn't it?

For her, there were four chimneys. That is the truth at the limits of the woman's knowledge, truth at a slant. The woman offered the

---

[53] Ibid., p. 4.

[54] See Marlene Kadar, "Resisting Holocaust Memory: Recuperating a Compromised Life," *The Memory Effect: The Remediation of Memory in Literature and Film*, ed. Russell J. A. Kilbourn and Eleanor Ty. Waterloo: WLUP, 2013. Pp. 125-141.

[55] See Dori Laub, "Bearing Witness, or the Vicissitudes of Listening."

Yale interviewers a backstory—what it truly "felt like" to be among others during the explosion, not all of what "really" happened.[56] The historians dismissed her version of the story as inaccurate because what we know from the history books is that only Crematorium IV blew up, at the deft hands of prisoners, men and women both, after which the brave were tortured, hanged, shot in the treed courtyard of Block 11. Crude bombs, they say.

We are scrupulous but rarely accurate, neither the survivors who remembered that it was only one chimney nor the witness who remembered four. Neither is Dori Laub, whose limits of knowledge had to shimmy in order to tell about a different truth. The historians must evade the memory of four chimneys. The historians had other interests. They wanted the truth; they did not want to know how the woman broke the frame of the memory of the truth of the rebellion. They had to foreclose on the deal and delete her story from the true one.

Between the worlds of the well and the unwell is the same irrevocable gap wherein the story lives and breathes with the fact of life. Between the well and the unwell is a huge chasm, an almost necessary silence, where the limits of knowledge shimmy. The unwell can never adopt the rules of behaviour prepared for healthy, sane people, even if they wear crutches. They cannot hurry to the office. They cannot eat the meals on tap. They can't go to the library when their skin bleeds, or their red blood cells cry. They can't even run a half marathon or jump a rope. What if their feet don't work? They may have a hard time satisfying the highest ethical standards established by the nonfiction police because the story of illness is not romantic or essentially happy and so they may lie or write about something that resembles a lie. They want to be happy and have every reason to be.

---

[56] I am indebted to the London-born Bangladeshi dancer and choreographer Akram Khan, who talks about his wish not to "make sense" but to "feel sense." *This Cultural Life*, Jan. 17, 2023, https://www.bbc.co.uk/programmes/w3ct4mnp..

There were indeed four chimneys, says the sick woman with lymphoma. I was there, I think. Yes, my memory is now flawed. I remember four bags of poisons that took seven hours to decant. That was on day one and there were many endless days if I do remember correctly now. Although I was guarded, I did not have to steal jewels.

What do we choose to tell each other? Sometimes we err on the side of historical and scientific "fact." Sometimes we don't. Who among us gets to go home? I do not always listen either, I guess, and yet I often think I do.

BIBLIOGRAPHY

Bindiger Cige, Marta. "Witness Statement from Marta Bindiger Cige." 19 Nov. 1945. *Anna Wajcblum Heilman's Diary written in Belgium (in Polish)*, Anna Heilman Fonds, Library and Archives Canada. R 11520. File 1–2 and File 2-23, http://central. bac-lac.gc.ca/.redirect?app=fonandcol&id=4478306&lang.

Bunch, Adam. "Emma Goldman in Toronto: One Last Victory for the Most Dangerous Woman in the World." *Spacing Toronto*, 12 Jan. 2016, www.spacing.ca/toronto/2016/01/12/53895/. Accessed 4 Dec. 2022.

Childers, Chad. "Neil Young Explains Songwriting: Never Chase the Rabbit." *UCR Classic Rock and Culture*, 12 June 2012, www.ultimateclassicrock.com/neil-young-explains-songwriting-never-chase-the-rabbit. Accessed 18 Dec. 2022.

Corkin, Jane, editor. *André Kertész: A Lifetime of Perception*. Key Porter Books, 1982.

"Dermatitis Herpetiformis." *Celiac Disease Foundation*, n.d., www.celiac.org/about-celiac-disease/related-conditions/dermatitis-herpetiformis/. Accessed 3 Dec. 2022.

Didion, Joan. "In Bed." *The White Album*. Farrar, Strauss and Giroux, 1979, pp. 168–72.

Dunsworth, Edward. "Green Gold, Red Threats: Organization and Resistance in Depression-Era Ontario Tobacco." *Labour/Le Travail*, vol. 79, 2017, pp. 105–42.

Eliot, George. *The Mill on the Floss*. 1860. Penguin Editions, 2003.

Epp, Stefan. "'Fighting for the Everyday Interests of Winnipeg Workers': Jacob Penner, Martin Forkin and the Communist Party in Winnipeg Politics, 1930–1935." *Manitoba History*, no. 63, Spring 2010. www.mhs.mb.ca/docs/mb-history/63/winnipeg-workers.shtml.

"'Finds Hitler and Cohorts World's Greatest Menace: Emma Goldman Calls upon Masses to Aid Germans Destroy Monster Dictator at Hygeia Hall' Article, Part 1 of 2." *Jewish Women's Archive*, n.d., https://jwa.org/media/article-about-goldmans-lecture-on-imminent-dangers-of-fascism-0.

Foucault, Michel. *The Birth of the Clinic: An Archaeology of Medical Perception*, translated by A. M. Sheridan Smith, Pantheon Books, 1973.

Freud, Sigmund. *Beyond the Pleasure Principle*. 1920. Translated by James Strachey, Dover Publications, 2015.

Goethe, Johann Wolfgang von. *Faust*, translated by Louis MacNeise, Faber & Faber, 2008.

Gottlieb, Amy. "Cancer Changed Me, but I'm Still the Same Person." *The Globe and Mail*, 11 Sep. 2022, www.theglobeandmail.com/life/first-person/article-cancer-changed-me-but-im-still-the-same-person/. Accessed 3 Dec. 2022.

Grossman, Ibolya Szalai. *An Ordinary Woman in Extraordinary Times*. Multicultural History Society of Ontario, 1990.

———, and Andy Réti. *Stronger Together*. The Azrieli Foundation, 2016.

Gulkin, Cathy, director. "A Glowing Dream: The Story of Jacob and Rose Penner." *A Scattering of Seeds*, season 2, episode 14. White Pine Pictures, 1998.

Gunn, Kirsty. *My Katherine Mansfield Project*. Notting Hill Editions, 2016.

"Heilman, Anna, Jewish Resistance Fighter (December 1, 1928–May 1, 2011)." *Ottawa Citizen*, 3 May 2011. Legacy.com, Obituaries, https://www.legacy.com/obituaries/ottawacitizen/obituary.aspx?n=anna-heilman&pid=150763418&fhid=5973. Accessed 16 Mar. 2023.

The Holy Bible: King James Version, n.d., www.kingjamesbible online.org/John-6-35/. Accessed Mar. 27, 2023.

Kadar, Marlene. "Resisting Holocaust Memory: Recuperating a Compromised Life," *The Memory Effect: The Remediation of*

Memory in Literature and Film, edited by Russell J. A. Kilbourn and Eleanor Ty, Wilfrid Laurier UP, 2013, pp. 125–41.

Kempis, Thomas à. *Of the Imitation of Christ: Four Books.* Oxford University Press, 1961.

Kennedy, Paul, and Barbara Nichol. "Dust to Dust: Notes on Rituals for the Dead." *Ideas*, CBC Radio, 6 Aug. 2018, https://www.cbc.ca/radio/ideas/dust-to-dust-notes-on-rituals-for-the-dead-1.3820687.

Khan, Akram, interview by John Wilson. *This Cultural Life*, BBC, 17 Jan. 2023. https://www.bbc.co.uk/programmes/w3ct4mnp.

Laub, Dori. "Bearing Witness, or the Vicissitudes of Listening." *Testimony: Crises of Witnessing in Literature, Psychoanalysis, and History*, edited by Shoshana Felman and Dori Laub, Routledge, 1992, pp. 57–74.

LCD Sound System. "New York, I Love You But You're Bringing Me Down." *Sound of Silver*, DFA Records, 2007.

Lederman, Marsha. *Kiss the Red Stairs: The Holocaust, Once Removed.* McClelland & Stewart, 2022.

Littell, Jonathan. *The Kindly Ones*, translated by Charlotte Mandell, McClelland & Stewart, 2010.

Moist, Paul. "A Walk through History: Brookside Cemetery Tours Feature Fascinating Figures Connected to Strike."" *The Free Press*, 1 June 2019, www.winnipegfreepress.com/local/2019/06/01/a-walk-through-history. Accessed 4 Dec. 2022.

Raab, Elisabeth M. *And Peace Never Came.* Wilfrid Laurier UP, 1997.

Rombauer, Irma S., and Marion Rombauer Becker. *The Joy of Cooking.* 1931. Thomas Allen and Son, 1972.

Rose, Jonathan. *The Intellectual Life of the British Working Classes.* 3rd ed., Yale University Press, 2001.

Salmi, Teea, and Kaisa Hervonen. "Current Concepts of Dermatitis Herpetiformis." *Medical Journals Sweden*, 6 Feb. 2020, www.medicaljournalssweden.se/actadv/article/download/1903/3295. Accessed 3 December 2022.

Sándor Lakatos and His Gypsy Band. "Keresek egy csendes zugot." *Magyar Nóták (Hungarian Popular Songs)*, Qualiton, 1964.

Seeburger, Frank. "Thinking Time, Drinking Time: A Beginner's Thought (3)." *Trauma and Philosophy*, n.d., www.traumaandphilosophy.wordpress.com/tag/trauma-and-addiction. Accessed 19 Sep. 2022.

Service, Robert William. "Grey Gull." *My Poetic Side*, n.d., www.mypoeticside.com/show-classic-poem-26202. Accessed 4 Dec. 2022.

Steinbeck, John. *The Pearl*. Vintage, 1947.

"Sten Gun." *Canadian Soldier*, n.d., www.canadiansoldiers.com/weapons/smgs/sten.htm. Accessed 4 Dec. 2022.

The American Influenza Epidemic of 1918–1919: A Digital Encyclopedia. "St. Louis, Missouri." University of Michigan Center for the History of Medicine and Michigan Publishing, n.d., www.influenzaarchive.org/cities/city-stlouis.html. Accessed 3 Dec. 2022.

Wolynn, Mark. *It Didn't Start with You: How Inherited Family Trauma Shapes Who We Are and How to End the Cycle*. Penguin Life, 2017.

ACKNOWLEDGEMENTS

"In the dark times / will there also be singing? / Yes, there will also be singing. / About the dark times."

Bertolt Brecht, 1939, quoted in "Reign of Embers" by Cecilia Woloch

Let's just say that all the singing going on props us all up and keeps us on course, too. I have many praises to sing, because I could not have approached my readers without a huge team of thinkers, writers, physicians, readers, editors, and lovers and beloveds.

The body has to come first in this song. I want to acknowledge the uniquely wise care I have received from a squad of devoted and sagacious physicians, some for more than a decade. It all started with the ingenious suspicions of Sandy Skotnicki in 2011 and 2012, then confirmed by a visionary in blood cancers, Michael Baker. Soon after began a long relationship with the gifted, patient, and forward-thinking Vishal Kukreti who, in tandem with Canada's prescient skin wizard Scott Walsh, persisted with my body's challenging presentations, revisiting each symptom with a quiet and yet certain manner. Relapse after worse relapse, including a failed stem cell transplant, until there was no standard of care remaining: Kukreti and Walsh never left me. As sometimes happens, a quirky immunological trial successfully got my very privileged blood cancer cells to return the body to an equilibrium. Tempted by the fates, squamous cell carcinoma invaded the left eye and upper face: MOHS physicians dug it out, and also dug out my left tear duct. Without a tear duct, one cannot write because the eye cries interminably, without a cause in nature or sorrow. Then came the artistry of Harmeet Gill and Sarah Lindsay who, with such kindness, sutured older skin with new life. Gill also installed a miracle: a Pyrex tear duct, a Jones Tube. Standing beside me all the way were Jennifer Viveiros, Fred Freedman, Liam O'Sullivan, and Phil Hébert. With the efforts of these extraordinary men and women, the link between body and pen was recovered. How can I ever thank them?

I also want to acknowledge others who have walked beside me all these years. There would be no book without Inanna Publications' Editor-in-Chief, Luciana Ricciutelli, whose last message to me connected my anxieties to hers in a soothing and productive way. "Just let it go," she said. I didn't think I could start again after Lu's death, but then appeared a dear friend to take the lead— Brenda Cranney. Brenda pushed me gently to let it go, as Luciana would have done, listening always for the things writers don't say, as if a silence could be published. Nobody remembers Lu better than Adebe DeRango-Adem *(https://poets.ca/luciana-ricciutelli-in-memoriam/)*, who pays tribute to how Luciana fiercely defended women and their words.

Inanna's team of editors, proofreaders, cover designer, and typesetter have made salient contributions to *Broken Fiction*. I don't know how to thank them. For her brilliant craft, her patient and creative editing, I want to thank Ashley Rayner, Senior Editor at Inkwell's Editorial Services. Rayner is exacting and yet always courteous and generous with her time and her advice. Ashley Rayner's skill with words is legendary, but she has the qualities of an editor I admire most: the desire to try things out, and the patience to change her mind when it is a better choice for the piece or for the flow of themes. Copyeditor Mel Mikhail has that special quality of respecting voice—mine, yes, of course, but also theirs. Mel and substantive editor Chelene Knight offered numerous revisions that improved the shape of the manuscript and the play of irony. Proofreader Meg Bowen caught my mistakes in good time, and Val Fullard fashioned a bright cover that boldly speaks back to Doris Wilson's rendering of the face and skin. Thanks also to the poetic Leigh Kotsilidis, talented and flexible typesetter.

Before editing, there must be writing. Writing, thinking, and love go together at the most opportune times. W3 (Deborah Barndt, Gail Lindsey, Barbara Rahder) and the Miners (Yvonne Singer and Belarie Zatzman) have inspired various collective projects for many years, as have the most generous readers, Ferne Cristall and Robert Clarke.

In this group of thinkers are my stellar former graduate students, now my colleagues, especially Eva Karpinski, Rachel Dubrofsky, and Mark Celinscak. Patrick Taylor, my colleague and friend, and I have walked and cycled side by side through thick and thin, culminating in the 2017 International Auto/biography Association conference where colleagues celebrated our work together: Eva Karpinski, Ricia Anne Chansky, Julie Rak, Jeanne Perreault, Elizabeth Podnieks, Sidonie Smith, Helen Buss, Susan Ingram, Linda Warley, Linda Morra, and remarkable others (*Life Writing Outside the Lines*, 2020).

We often remember those who live down the street and who, in their way, made things happen when the subject was herself failing. I want to acknowledge the quiet efforts of heroic intelligence by Amila Butorović, Joan Steigerwald, Celia Haig-Brown, Madiha Didi Khayatt, Reva Marin, Matthew Clark, Jan Rehner, and Arun P. Mukherjee. I cannot measure their ability to stay while also proceeding, moving on without forgetting, inviting me out as if I was a normal person waiting for a car mechanic.

I have made up another family that I pretend is connected by blood when really it is only love: Mary Ellen Marus (her weekly gifts and cards are a treasure trove of comic subjects), Steve Penner;

Shaena Lambert (and *Oh, My Darling*, 2014), Bob Penner; Douglas Freake, Linda Sutherland; Glynnis French, Robert French, and Robin Fairfull-Smith; Lee Davis Creal and Michael Creal; Doreen Balabanoff and Stuart Reid; Yvonne Singer and Ron Singer; Michael Kaufman, Debbie Field, David Kraft, Victoria Lee, Amy Gottlieb, and Maureen Fitzgerald. Their magic works over and over again. As tedious as this journey has sometimes been, they hang on, often with humour, good food, great stories, Mary Meyer overalls, and martinis. This is especially true of the woman who has taught me so much as we walked across the dais, or as we strolled in High Park or in Vondelpark: Susan Ehrlich.

The same is true for cousins Cathy Gulkin, who keeps the Jewish holidays alive for all of us; and Lisa Simkins, Mike Green, Ellen Lipes, Myra Lipes, Howard Wolpert who have brought great change to the world in their work, but also in my life. Their devotion has contributed to a very good life, well or unwell.

There were those whose focus on change in the world inspired me as a young scholar, and gave me courage. I will never forget early role models: Ella Wolfe who told me about Frida Kahlo and her letters ("peel me a grape") at the Hoover Institution of War, Revolution and Peace; Jean van Heijenoort, Trotsky's multilingual secretary, who told me there was a Canadian in the Trotsky archives at Harvard's Houghton Library and guided me through the previously closed sections of the papers to find him. The "Canadian" turned out to be Earle Robertson, aka poet and novelist Earle Birney. "Van" and Earle shared a secret job: they both carried revolvers to protect Leon Trotsky in exile. To this fierce tradition, I hitched my wagon, as did many others at the time.

The penultimate verse is for the ones who are always around and can't really leave even if they want to: diehard family sages, cooks, comedians, and chauffeurs. They waited patiently; they were generous with their time and their love; they brought me gifts from *Friends NYC* and other Brooklyn haunts; they built things for me; they decorated my world. From the bottom of my heart, I want to thank Jacob Kadar Penner, Kimberley Bruce, Emma Kadar Penner, Jayson Green, and the wise and loving Gary Galaxy, whose guitar once again sings through the vents as I write. But not always about the dark times.

Finally, my parents, Helen and Joe Kadar, Norma and Norman Penner, Mary and Art Pidgeon; and grandparents, George and Marcela Bednarik and Vasel and Margarette Kadar. It didn't all start with me, but it did start in the Junction. I have not gotten very far from them, I guess.

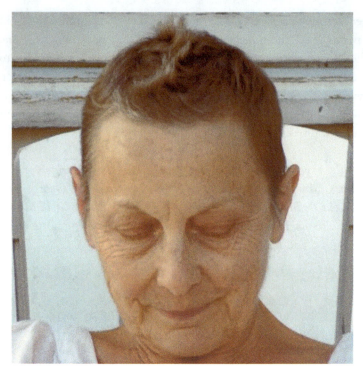

Marlene Kadar is a writer who lives in Toronto. She is also Professor Emerita and Senior Scholar at York University. She studies domestic archival artefacts, including photographs. She is the Founding Editor of the Life Writing Series at Wilfrid Laurier University Press.